A sho
across the night sky

Genie let out a little gasp, staring in awe at the brilliant trail of light. "Did you see that?" she whispered, turning her eyes toward Byron as an involuntary shiver went through her.

"Lovely." Byron's voice was low and husky.

Their eyes met and held in spite of the darkness, and for a moment Genie had the incredible impression that the phosphorescent brightness of the meteorite's trail was filling the space between them.

"Genie, would you do something for me?" Byron said at last.

"What?"

"Go back into the house and close the door and lock it."

Katherine Arthur is full of life. She describes herself as a writer, research associate (she works with her husband, a research professor in experimental psychology), farmer, housewife, proud mother of five and a grandmother to boot. The family is definitely full of overachievers. But what she finds most interesting is the diversity of occupations the children have chosen—sports medicine, computers, finance and neuroscience (pioneering brain tissue transplants), to name a few. Why, the possibilities for story ideas are practically limitless.

Books by Katherine Arthur

HARLEQUIN ROMANCE
2991—THROUGH EYES OF LOVE
3014—LOVING DECEIVER
3043—MOUNTAIN LOVESONG
3061—ONE MORE SECRET
3103—TO TAME A COWBOY
3181—KEEP MY HEART FOREVER

SIGNS OF LOVE
Katherine Arthur

Harlequin Books

TORONTO • NEW YORK • LONDON
AMSTERDAM • PARIS • SYDNEY • HAMBURG
STOCKHOLM • ATHENS • TOKYO • MILAN
MADRID • WARSAW • BUDAPEST • AUCKLAND

ISBN 0-373-03229-3

Harlequin Romance first edition November 1992

SIGNS OF LOVE

CHAPTER ONE

THE MORNING SUN filtered weakly through the wisps of early fog that clung like cobwebs to the mountainside. The far edge of the yard below the deck where Genie Compton and her nephew, Tim Donaldson, stood was blurred, the green of the lawn and the normally bright colors of the azaleas resembling an Impressionist painting by Monet. Lower down, past the high board fence, the wisps became swirling billows of fog that obscured the base of the mountain from view, leaving the mountaintop residents floating in mysterious isolation.

"Can't see very far, can you?" Genie commented, looking down at Tim.

The five-year-old had his chin propped on the railing of the deck as he stared into the fog. He turned his head and rolled huge dark eyes up toward her. "I thought I saw a monster out there. D'you think there could be one? A sea monster?" His voice became more excited. "It might come galumphing up the mountain in the fog and get us!"

Genie smiled at him and smoothed his dark hair back affectionately. "I don't think I'd worry about it. I grew up in this house, and we never had one sea monster attack us. But if one does decide to stroll up this way, I hope it climbs carefully over Grandpa's fence and jumps over Grandma's flower beds. They'd be awfully mad if a sea monster ruined their pretty garden." She hoped that her answer was fanciful enough for Tim. Tim was adopted, but his vivid

imagination was so like her sister, Portia's, that Genie
sometimes felt hard-pressed to keep up with it.

Genie tended to see things in much more realistic terms.
She knew that later, when the sun rose higher, the fog
would burn away to reveal no sea monsters but only the
narrow strip of highway, commercial buildings and sandy
beach below and, beyond, the ever-changing blue of the
Pacific. It was, she thought now, one of those strange
spring mornings in Southern California, more like North-
ern California really, here so close to the ocean. Inland, it
was probably already warm and sunny. At the Heavenly
Valley Tennis Club, where she was one of the staff profes-
sionals, it could easily be a blistering ninety degrees by this
afternoon.

"I'd just as soon stay here with you, Ms. Kitty," Genie
said to the ample mother cat who came to curl around her
legs, purring loudly.

"And I'd just as soon play with the kittens," said Tim,
crouching to pick up the first in the line of six progeny that
came waddling along in pursuit of their mother. "I want
this guy to take home. He's the toughest. I'm gonna call
him Monster." He stood up, cuddling a fat yellow tom-
kitten against his cheek.

"In another week or so," Genie said, "if it's all right
with your mother."

"It will be," Tim said confidently, and Genie knew he
was right. Portia would cope in her own inimitable way. If
something disturbed her screwball but serene life, she
would simply consult her current guru. If that didn't help,
she would put it down to cosmic forces that would eventually reveal their purpose to her and let it go at that.

Genie often envied her sister's ability to make the best of
almost any situation. At the moment, there was no way she
could imagine herself looking forward to the day ahead. It

was Saturday. She had a full schedule of lessons with people who had to work during the week. But, she thought with a sigh, she was in no mood to face another day of correcting flubbed backhands and jerky serves. It was so peaceful here. When her parents had asked if she would mind house-sitting while they were in England for her father's sabbatical from the university, she had jumped at the chance. And right now she could think of nothing more pleasant than curling up on the big, comfortable redwood lounge on the deck with a good book while Tim played with the kittens or built them a house with his blocks. They could have lunch at the umbrella-shaded table, and then go to the beach in the afternoon.

She sighed again. This was definitely not the time for that fantasy to come true. She not only had to get through the day, but she had to put in an appearance tonight at the special dedication party, in honor of opening the new wing at the club. Grover Aldrich, the austere, graying president of the club, would take a dim view of anyone who was not practically at death's door missing that event, and Portia and her husband, Mark, co-chairpersons of the party, would be even more upset. It was to give them the previous evening for the final preparations that she had brought Tim home with her to spend the night.

"We'd better be going, Tim," she said. She bent to give Ms. Kitty a caress. "Take good care of those kittens while I'm gone." She shouldered her purse strap, picked up the small suitcase that contained her outfit for the party, then hurried down the steps from the deck and through the door to the carport.

She put her suitcase into the trunk, then flung her purse into the back seat of her little white convertible.

"Fasten your seat belt," she said to Tim.

"I always do," he said, frowning at her reprovingly as he clicked it into place.

"Good for you," Genie said. She turned the key. The car gave a rasping cough to protest the dampness.

"Come on, car," Tim encouraged.

Genie nodded in agreement. "I sure don't want to have to call the garage to start it." The car responded by coughing once more and then settling into a comfortably steady hum.

"Good car," Tim said, and Genie smiled at the way he encouraged it as if it were human. She had been known to speak to it herself, but only when it misbehaved. She shifted into reverse and backed up the short steep driveway to the road. She paused, looking carefully both ways. She could see nothing threatening in either direction and began to back across the nearest lane so that she could turn and head down the mountain to the Coast Highway. Her front tires had not even cleared the driveway when the blast of a horn tore the air behind her, rubber screeched loudly against the pavement and the sharp jolt of impact shook the car.

A rush of adrenaline wiped out Genie's earlier torpor. She jammed on her brakes and jerked her head around just in time to see a black Ferrari go speeding on down the hill.

"You insane idiot!" she yelled, her heart pounding. "What in heaven's name were you doing on my side of the street?" She looked quickly over at Tim, who was staring at her, wide-eyed. "Are you all right?" she asked.

"Sure," he replied. "Are you?"

"I am, but my car isn't," Genie growled. "And that... that crazy fool didn't even stop!" She grated into first gear and pulled her car back into the driveway. "You stay in— I'm just going to look at it," she said to Tim as she leaped out to inspect the damage.

"Oh, no!" she moaned. "Never had a scratch before, and now I'll probably have to have the whole fender redone." It had been only a glancing blow, but the taillight cover was broken, there was a small dent and several streaks of black paint. Visions of either a bill for hundreds of dollars or skyrocketing insurance premiums danced before her tear-filled eyes. She was still bent over, inspecting the spot with her fingertips, when she heard another screech of tires some distance down the hill, and then the heavy, pulsing roar of a powerful engine coming back toward her. "He'd better stop, or I'll chase him until I catch him," Genie muttered, peering down the street, her eyes narrowed. The street dead-ended at the top of the mountain, and there was no way he could escape, even in that car.

The Ferrari came into view, speeding as before. Genie stood, hands planted on her hips, watching. The car gave no sign of slowing until it was almost upon her, then suddenly skittered to a noisy stop. A coiled mass of muscular male sprang from the car and advanced on her, dark eyes flashing beneath an angry scowl. The man was wearing faded jeans and a sleeveless T-shirt spattered with splotches of paint, his shoulder-length mahogany-colored hair held in place by a rolled red bandanna tied around his head. This poorly dressed apparition, Genie noted with a rising tide of anger that evaporated her tears and made her cheeks feel hot, did not appear either embarrassed or apologetic. His square jaw was set and his brows were drawn together above a nose that looked as if it had been broken more than once. He looked, to Genie's critical eye, more like a beach bum who ended up in frequent brawls than the driver of an expensive car. But then, in Southern California she knew that you could expect almost anything, even that someone who had just smashed into your car would glare at you as if it was your fault!

"Do you always drive like a madman, or am I just especially lucky?" Genie demanded, preempting the expected accusation.

"Neither," the man replied in an ice-dripping growl. "Don't you look before you back out into the street?"

"Yes," she growled back, "but I wasn't looking for a rocket. You were nowhere in sight when I started to back out, so don't try to pin the blame on me. You were driving much too fast and you were on my side of the street."

"The hell I was," the man roared. "It was you or the neighbor's mailbox." He gave Genie's fender a cursory glance. "You didn't see me coming, did you?" he said, lifting his chin arrogantly, his dark eyes glittering with contempt as he slowly scanned Genie, from her mane of sun-streaked hair, down her slender frame in a trim blue warm-up suit, to her bare, sandal-clad feet.

"I saw a speck in the distance," Genie retorted, jerking her own chin up and giving him a similar, cold-eyed inspection that she hoped revealed her contempt for his slovenly appearance. "The next thing I knew, you'd hit me. Let's just see if you left some tire marks on the pavement. On my side of the street!" She marched past the man, giving him a contemptuous glare as she passed. "Look at that," she said, pointing to a black streak. "You were a mile from the neighbor's mailbox."

"You can't prove that my car made that mark," the man said, frowning still.

I've got him now. He knows he did it, Genie thought with grim satisfaction, watching the man's face. He no longer looked nearly as sure of himself. "Want to bet?" she retorted. "I'll bet forensics can match the rubber. How fast were you going, anyway?"

The man shrugged off her question, now looking stoically resigned. "I was in a hurry. All right, let's pretend I was the one to blame. I don't have time to argue." He reached into his back pocket, pulled out his billfold and took out a small white card. "Here," he said, handing it to Genie. "If you have something to write with, I'll give you my telephone number. Get a couple of estimates and let me know how much you need."

"No insurance?" Genie asked caustically.

"Plenty, but I'd rather handle this myself," the man replied quietly. "Don't worry, I'm good for it, and I won't skip town. I live in the last house at the top of the hill."

Genie shrugged, took the card without looking at it, then reached for her purse and found a pen. "All right," she said, holding the card against her car with its blank side toward her.

The man gave her a number and then added, "Would you mind telling me your name so I'll know who you are when you call?"

"Why? Do you have so many accidents that you have trouble keeping all of the claims straight?" Genie asked. Anger flashed across the man's face again, and she shivered involuntarily. He looked as if he would like to hit her. "Eugenia Compton," she replied stiffly.

She put the pen away and turned the card over, trying to hide her surprise at the name she saw. "Byron de Stefano, Paintings and Serigraphs" was the legend engraved on the card. That name was certainly familiar enough to her. There had been a flap between the elders of the club that lasted for weeks when the famous artist was commissioned to do a large painting for the new club lounge, some of them preferring a more realistic style than that for which de Stefano was known. She remembered now Mark's mentioning that he lived up the road from the Compton house, but it was still rather hard to digest the fact that this person, who looked like a caricature of a Bohemian artist, was, in fact, the real thing. "Thank you, Mr. de Stefano," she said as coolly as she could, slowly raising her eyes to meet his. "I'll be in touch as soon as I get some estimates. I won't be able to do that until next Monday at the earliest."

Byron de Stefano nodded but made no move to leave. He studied Genie seriously for so long that she began to feel uncomfortable. Then he looked over at Tim and his eyes narrowed, a strange, intensely concentrated look coming over his face. His gaze shifted back and forth several times, then settled on Genie again. He appeared about to speak when Tim, who was on his knees on the car seat watching the scene, broke the silence.

"Are you a pirate?" he asked.

The startled look on Byron de Stefano's face and the jerky movement of his head as he turned to look back at Tim made Genie wonder if he'd thought the boy couldn't speak. But he recovered quickly and smiled, his white teeth dazzling against his swarthy skin.

"That's right," he said, "but I traded my ship in for that car." He jerked his thumb toward the Ferrari.

Tim grinned, obviously aware that they were sharing a joke. "That's a neat car," he said.

"Thanks." Byron de Stefano's smile faded and he returned his attention to Genie. "I don't remember seeing you or your boy around here before. Are you new here?" he asked.

Genie shook her head. "No. I lived here most of my life. This is my parents' house. I've lived elsewhere for some time."

"I see," said Byron de Stefano. He frowned, as if in deep thought. "Eugenia Compton. It seems to me I remember that name."

"I doubt it," Genie replied. There was something about the intensity of Byron de Stefano's dark eyes that made her feel very uncomfortable. She glanced quickly at her watch. "I'd better be going," she said. "I'll get that taken care of as soon as possible." She gestured toward her car.

Byron de Stefano nodded and then walked over to look at her damaged fender more closely. "Not too bad," he said, straightening from his inspection. "I am sorry. I hope you realize that you scared the hell out of me, backing out like that." When Genie made no reply, he looked at Tim. "Tell your mother to drive more carefully from now on."

Before Genie could splutter out an enraged reply, Tim piped up, "She's not my mom, she's my aunt."

"Mmm," said Byron de Stefano, lifting one dark brow and giving Genie another quick appraisal. "Married?" he asked.

"None of your business!" Genie snapped. She turned her back on him and got into her car. She intended to slam the door firmly after herself, but Byron had taken hold of it. He closed it gently.

"I remember where I saw your name," he said, bending toward her. "You're a pro at the Heavenly Valley Tennis Club, aren't you?"

Genie glared at him. "Yes, and I'm going to be late for my first lesson, thanks to you," she said coldly.

Byron de Stefano grinned. "Drive carefully," he said, then turned and walked away. Moments later, he wheeled his Ferrari around and started back down the mountain at a much slower pace.

"Infuriating man," Genie muttered as she started her car again.

"Why didn't you want him to know you aren't married?" Tim asked.

"Because it's none of his business," Genie replied. "Besides, I didn't like the way he looked at me."

"Like a pirate?"

That, Genie thought, was very apt. "Yes," she agreed, "like a pirate." Definitely predatory. Not at all what she would have expected from a man who was said to be a virtual recluse. There had been another brouhaha recently when Byron de Stefano adamantly refused to come to the party tonight for the unveiling of his painting. The story had passed around that he never attended such events, in fact seldom went out in public since he had moved to his mountaintop retreat in Laguna Beach some years ago. He had come from somewhere in the East, after his wife and child were killed in a tragic accident. No one seemed to know the details, but they had been quick to criticize him for disappointing them. High time, they said, for the man to return to the real world and discharge his responsibilities as a famous artist should. Genie had felt sympathetic at the time, picturing him as pale and wan and sorrowful looking. Now, she doubted that he was nearly as reclusive as he would like people to think. He looked far too healthy, and the gleam in his eyes was not that of a man who wanted for female companionship. Apparently he'd had time to recover from his grief.

Genie sighed and bit her lip. How long, she wondered, did it take to forget? Since her fiancé, Kurt Wallis, had died in a deep-sea diving accident last year she had felt much of the time as if she was only going through the motions of living. Portia and Mark had done their best recently to get her to begin to date again, but she could not bring herself to do so. Portia even theorized that her eagerness to return to the home of their childhood was something like an attempt to retreat to the womb during the hours when she was not at work. For a change, Genie had not argued with her sister's attempts at psychoanalysis. For all she knew, she might be right. She felt comfortable in her old room, her old bed. The idea of going out with someone new repelled her. When that feeling might change, she had no idea. So far, all of her attempts to make it go away had failed.

Being forcibly reminded of something that she was trying so hard to forget made Genie feel depressed and irritable. Why couldn't the person who smashed into her car have been some little Yuppie stockbroker in an Italian suit and a Rolex watch instead of the blatantly individualistic Byron de Stefano? Kurt had been unconventional, too, his long blond hair sometimes unkempt, his body muscular and deeply tanned from hours at sea. He had been a marine biologist with a brilliant career ahead of him. Not only had she lost the man she loved, but the world had lost someone valuable. It wasn't fair, she thought for the millionth time, tears pricking at her eyes.

By the time Genie turned into the plush grounds of the Heavenly Valley Tennis Club and parked in her assigned space, she was trembling with a combination of anger at herself for her weakness and the entire cosmos for its unfairness.

"There's Mom!" Tim said as soon as they stopped, unbuckling his seat belt and jumping out to run toward her.

"So she is," Genie said with a sigh. She never ceased to be amazed at the sight of her sister. A full head shorter than Genie and considerably heavier, Portia Donaldson always dressed in flowing, bright-colored clothes, multiple chains of gold and silver around her neck and rows of bangles on her arms. She reminded Genie of a colorful, round bird, who floated along the ground instead of flying.

As Genie watched, she enveloped Tim in a hug and then hurried toward her. "Have a good time?" she asked.

"Fine, until this morning," Genie replied. "An idiot in a Ferrari crunched my fender when I was backing out of the driveway."

"He looked like a pirate," Tim put in. "He was neat."

"Well, for goodness' sake," said Portia, shaking her head at the damaged fender. "Who was it? Didn't he even stop?"

Genie grimaced. She hated to tell Portia, who would doubtless pass the word around that Byron de Stefano was not in permanent seclusion and make the members even more angry at his refusal to come. But then, why should she care? He deserved it. "You'll never believe it," she said, "but it was Byron de Stefano himself. I hope he paints better than he drives."

"Byron..." Portia's eyes opened wide. "Oh, my. This may be very significant."

"Significant?" As usual, Portia's leaps of logic left Genie baffled. "What do you mean, significant?"

"Don't you realize," Portia said seriously, "what precise timing it took for you two to collide just so in that particular spot? That took celestial planning."

Genie shook her head. "It wasn't celestial planning. It was Byron de Stefano driving too fast and not staying on his side of the road. Now, I've got to hurry or I'm going to be late. See you later." She grabbed her suitcase, slammed the trunk of her car shut and ran at a trot into the locker room. Celestial planning! Where did Portia get such notions? If there was any planning involved, she would put her money on the devil's being the perpetrator! Her locker door stuck as usual, and she had just administered a resounding kick to the bottom edge when she heard a familiar voice behind her.

"Having a bad morning, Genie?"

"Oh, no, just having trouble with this door again," Genie said, recognizing the voice of Mimi Robards, her first pupil for the day. She took a deep breath, then turned to give her a bright smile. There was no point in taking her frustrations out on her pupils. "How are you today,

Mimi?'' she asked as she stripped off her warm-up suit and slipped into one of her simple tennis dresses. "Ready to tackle that top-spin lob?"

"I think so. I've been trying it on my own," the young girl replied.

They fell into easy conversation about tennis while Genie finished dressing and then checked her appointment book. Although she had been reluctant earlier, now she was happy to confirm that she was booked solid, except for a half-hour break morning and afternoon, plus an hour for lunch. She would have little time to brood about her car, or her encounter with the aggravating Byron de Stefano.

By her afternoon break, Genie's enthusiasm was beginning to wane. In spite of her best efforts to concentrate on her pupils, her earlier edginess did not go away, and several times she had to bite her tongue to keep from making an unpleasant remark when her instructions were not carried out as quickly as she would like. As four-thirty neared she fervently hoped that her last pupil, her brother-in-law, Mark, would decide to take the day off to rest up for the party. She was fond of him, and he was one of her best students, but she was so tired and tense that she ached from head to foot. Nevertheless she managed a smile when he appeared, moving at a trot from the direction of the locker room. Mark was an easygoing, friendly man, sandy haired and a bit stout, whose down-to-earth common sense and warm personality endeared him to everyone. He was, Genie knew, a perfect foil for her eccentric sister.

"Slow down," she said when he reached her side. "I'm not in any hurry."

Mark grinned. "I've been hurrying all day. I need a good session to relax me."

"I'll give you a good workout," Genie promised, wishing that she had some hope that it would relax her. "Anything special you want to work on?"

"My backhand down the line, as usual," he replied. "Tried to get one past Grover Aldrich when he came to the net yesterday and it sailed out a mile."

Genie laughed. "He's got awfully long arms. Maybe you tried too hard. Okay, let's work on that. Let's warm up a little first."

They took positions on opposite sides of the net and began hitting the ball back and forth at a good clip. Mark really had improved, Genie thought with satisfaction as his shots came back, solidly hit. "Okay," she said at last, picking up a caddy of balls, "let's try some of those backhands. Get those shoulders turned right away and get your foot planted firmly."

Mark complied and sent several powerful strokes sailing down the sideline.

"Excellent," Genie commended him. "Now let's try it when you have to move a little farther."

The rest of the half hour went quickly. "I do enjoy teaching someone who learns so quickly," Genie said as they left the court.

Mark beamed. "Thanks, coach. I only wish I'd had your help when I was starting out. Then I wouldn't have had so many bad habits to unlearn. You all set for the big party tonight? Got a pretty new dress?"

Genie made a face. "Yes, brother-in-law. I'll be there, looking sweet and demure if it kills me."

"Sweet and demure?" Mark laughed heartily. "Who are you trying to kid? I'd like to have heard you when de Stefano ran into you this morning. Portia told me all about it."

"I was quite restrained," Genie said reprovingly. "Tim was with me."

"That's right, he was," Mark said, still chuckling. "I wish I had been. I'd sure like to meet that man. In my humble opinion, he's a genius. I tried my best to convince him to come tonight, at least as well as I could by letter. He has an unlisted phone. I even drove up to his house once. It's a beautiful place, set way back in the trees. Did you ever see it?"

Genie shook her head.

"I walked all around it. I guess he wasn't home, because I didn't see his car. I was kind of surprised when Portia said he drives a Ferrari. That sounds more like a swinger than a recluse."

"He looks more like one, too," Genie said, "except that he has long hair and dresses like a beach bum. Maybe he's one of those artists who only communicates with a small circle of similar types." She thought momentarily of giving his phone number to Mark, but quickly decided against it. Even though she would like to help Mark, it was not her place to reveal something the artist did not want known. Besides, she didn't really want to see him again. If it weren't for him, she would have had a much more pleasant day.

"Could be," Mark replied with a sigh. "Well, I've got to go home and get cleaned up so I don't look like a bum myself. See you a little later."

By five-thirty the club had become almost ghostly quiet as the membership left to put on their formal finery while the staff prepared for the banquet, scheduled for seven o'clock. Genie took a shower and then stretched out in her terry robe on a sofa in the women's lounge, trying without much success to relax until it was time to get dressed. Shortly after six she abandoned the effort and began to put on her makeup. She went all the way, with foundation, eyeshadow, mascara, blusher and lipstick, knowing full well that if she didn't Portia would scold her for not trying to look her best. That done, she took her dress from the closet where one of the maids had hung it after giving it a final pressing. All of her old dresses reminded her of some special time she had spent with Kurt, so she had bought herself a new one of soft blue voile that brought out the blue of her eyes and complemented her deep tan. It was conservatively cut, with a modest scooped neckline and capelike sleeves, but Genie had to admit to herself that with her face carefully made up, her hair flowing loose to her shoulders and faux diamonds sparkling in her ears, she did not look like someone who had withdrawn from life. It was going to be harder than ever to persuade several of the single men that she simply was not interested in dating them.

Genie waited until the last minute before going into the new dining room and finding her place, for she knew that Grover Aldrich had planned the seating and would doubtless have put her at a table with some of those single men, probably Fred Martin and Bob Welch. The club president was a prominent psychiatrist who didn't hesitate to give unasked-for advice. He had recently joined Mark and Portia's chorus, urging her to start acting more like a beautiful young woman instead of an old woman in mourning, and Fred and Bob seemed to be at the top of his list for renewing her interest in men.

She quickly discovered that she was right about her tablemates, and that Grover, Portia and Mark were all at the next table. This, she thought grimly, looked like a conspiracy. She could see Portia darting quick glances at her from the corner of her eye, while Mark, who was more or less facing her, smiled like an overfed pussycat every time she looked his way. She managed to keep a smile plastered on her face and listen to her companions attentively enough to be able to carry on a conversation. But it was tiring, and she was relieved when the after-dinner speeches were over and the entire roomful of members adjourned to the new lounge for the unveiling of Byron de Stefano's painting while the dining room was made ready for the dance to follow.

The furniture in the lounge had been arranged so that about half of the members could sit and watch, while the rest stood in semicircular rows behind them. Genie declined an invitation to sit on the arm of Fred Martin's chair and stood behind it, instead. Mark was to have the honor of pulling the cord to uncover the painting, but he was nowhere in sight. Grover Aldrich went to the front of the group and stood looking over the heads of the crowd toward the doorway.

"I believe we're to have an unexpected honor tonight," he said. "Ah, yes, there they come."

Genie almost laughed at the way everyone's head immediately swiveled around. Then a murmur went through the crowd and she felt a sudden constriction in her throat as she recognized the words she heard over and over—"de Stefano." She turned her head then, to find Byron de Stefano looking directly at her. After a moment he turned away to answer a question from Mark, walking at his side, but she could not stop looking at him. He wore no headband tonight, his shiny dark hair falling back from his face in deep, lush waves. He wore a loose white gauze shirt with an open neck and full sleeves, and tight black leather pants. The total effect of those simple clothes was stunning, accenting the breadth of his thickly muscled shoulders and the trimness of his hips. "He looks like a Gypsy," she heard a woman whisper. "Or a pirate," said another. "So romantic," said a third. The faces of the men nearby, when Genie finally tore her eyes away, were set and inscrutable. Clearly, their expressions told her, Byron de Stefano had upstaged all of them in their formal finery.

Grover Aldrich said something that caused the audience to applaud, and Mark took the microphone and said a few words, but Genie could not have told anyone what was said. As soon as Byron de Stefano had reached the front of the room he had again sought her out with his eyes, and she could do nothing but stare back at him, while her heart pounded so loudly in her ears that it drowned out all but the loudest sounds. At last he looked away to acknowledge another round of applause from the audience with gracious but unsmiling nods. Hands clenched tightly at her sides, Genie felt like fleeing while she was still able, but knew that she would make a fool of herself if she did. She bit her lip and watched, her head swimming, as Mark finally reached for the cord that held the cover over the huge painting. A hush fell over the crowd. Genie knew that Byron was watching her again, but she dared not look at him. Instead, she waited, scarcely breathing, for the curtain to fall away.

When it did, she could feel herself inhale sharply, and a warm flush crept over her as a swell of applause swept across the room. "Magnificent," she heard someone say, and she agreed wordlessly. Somehow, Byron de Stefano's bold, vivid strokes conveyed motion, grace, beauty and competitive strife in a way that she had never imagined before. Forms were not defined, and yet they were there, shifting and changing even as she looked. A genius, Mark had said. He was right, she thought. But why had Byron de Stefano decided to come tonight? And the way he stared at her! What did he want? Timidly she turned her eyes back toward him, but people were standing between them now, and she could not see him. He might be coming toward her. What would she say to him? Why did just the thought of talking to him make her throat feel tight and her heart pound?

"Ready to try out the dance floor? I hear the orchestra tuning up back in the dining room." Bob Welch appeared at Genie's side, smiling.

"Uh, maybe in a few minutes," she replied, trying to smile back. "I'm going to the powder room first." With that lame excuse, she turned and fled.

The elegant new powder room did not provide Genie with the refuge she sought. Several other women were there, including Grover Aldrich's stylish wife, Dorothy, who immediately began a nonstop conversation with Genie. "You look so lovely tonight. How did you like the painting? Isn't Byron gorgeous?" She kept it up until Genie had fidgeted with her hair and makeup as long as she could, then actively took hold of Genie's arm and propelled her back toward the festivities.

Her suspicions of a conspiracy confirmed, Genie desperately tried to think of some avenue of escape. To her relief, almost everyone was dancing when they reached the room. "I think I'll get some punch," she said, finally shaking her arm loose from Dorothy's viselike grip. She hurried toward the refreshment bar, then veered quickly off through the doorway into the lounge, hoping to find respite there. One step into the room and she came to a quick halt. Byron de Stefano was still standing near his painting, talking to her sister and brother-in-law. She was about to beat another hasty retreat when both Mark and Byron spotted her. Mark smiled and beckoned to her, but it was Byron's intense gaze that drew her across the intervening space like, she thought helplessly, an iron filing to a magnet.

"This is my sister-in-law, Genie Compton," Mark said, his eyes twinkling devilishly. "I believe you two, uh, ran into each other earlier today." Mark threw back his head and laughed uproariously at his own joke.

Genie shot him a dark look, then glanced up at Byron. "Hello again," she said.

"Ms. Compton," Byron said gravely, extending his hand. "I believe I prefer this introduction."

"Uh, yes," Genie said, wishing fervently that there were some way she could avoid taking Byron's hand without appearing rude. Somehow, the idea of touching him terrified her. But there was no way to avoid it. His long fingers closed around her strong, tanned hand, warm and possessive in their pressure. When he did not release her hand, Genie tried to pull it away, but his grasp was firm and she could do no more without appearing conspicuous. She stood there, staring into Byron's eyes, feeling the warmth seeping up her arm and wondering madly if there would be a brand in the shape of Byron de Stefano's fingers on her hand when he took it away. She could feel Mark and Portia staring at her, probably wondering if she'd been struck dumb. Desperate for something intelligent to say, she looked past Byron to the painting behind him, but could think of nothing better than some trite remark about how wonderful it was, and so she remained silent.

"I'm glad you like it," Byron said, breaking the silence.

Genie looked back at him, startled, her eyes wide.

"I was watching your face when Mark pulled the cord," he said, the faintest hint of a smile at the corners of his mouth.

"It...it's wonderful," Genie said, feeling foolish as she did so. The word was totally inadequate to describe her impression.

"Thank you," Byron said, as seriously as if she had just given him a really intelligent comment. "I only wish that I could create something as lovely as you. I'm surprised that you could escape the dance floor for a second look at my painting."

At that extravagant compliment, Genie blushed scarlet. "You're . . . too kind," she murmured.

"Most of the men here would agree with you, Byron," Mark said, his eyes dancing mischievously, "but Genie's very elusive. They're not sure she even knows how to dance."

Genie glared at him, but he looked back at her with a bland smile. She saw Portia raise her eyebrows and her bright blue eyes dart quickly back and forth between her and Byron.

"But I do know how to dance," Portia said, developing a mischievous smile of her own. She put her arm through her husband's. "I think they're playing our song. Come along, dear."

"Duty calls," Mark said affably. "If you'll excuse us..."

Our song, my foot, Genie thought crossly as Portia and Mark abandoned her. She tried again to tug her hand free, but Byron only held on more tightly. She looked up at him pleadingly, feeling dizzy and stupidly frightened.

"Shall we find out whether you can dance?" he suggested softly. "I assure you, I dance better than I drive." He finally smiled, a gentle little smile that sent flickering lights dancing deep in his eyes.

Entranced, Genie could only say weakly, "All right, but I'm afraid I play tennis much better than I dance," and then try to calm her tightening nerves as Byron put his hand at her waist as if they were already dancing, and led her into the dining room. At the edge of the dance floor he paused and turned Genie into his arms, taking a firm grip on her hand.

"Relax," he commanded, then pulled her close.

Relax? Genie was too numb to tell whether she was relaxed or not. She vaguely thanked God that Byron was very skilled at leading, for her knees felt like wobbly jelly, and

above them her only sensation was of the warmth of Byron's hard male body fitted snugly against hers as if they
were interlocking pieces of a puzzle. The first dance was
slow, and they moved together wordlessly, Byron's head
lowered so that his cheek barely touched Genie's forehead.
She gradually became conscious of other sensations, the
soft heathery smell of his hair, the thin, rough feel of his
shirt between her hand and the hard muscles of his back,
the rhythm of the dance that pulsed both in her ears and
between them.

When the music stopped, he did not release her. She
looked up at him questioningly.

"You dance beautifully," he said simply, then tightened
his grip as the orchestra began an old-fashioned waltz. They
began to turn in sweeping curves in time to the rhythm, as
many of the couples left the floor.

It was, Genie thought wonderingly, almost like flying.
She felt as if her feet were scarcely touching the floor. Suddenly she became aware that they were almost alone on the
dance floor. Her step faltered. "Sorry," she said, embarrassed. "I just noticed that everyone's staring at us."

"Not surprising," Byron replied just as the waltz came
to an end. "Let's get some air." His arm still encircling her,
he ushered Genie quickly through the crowd and out onto
the wide terrace, where colorful round tables were filled
with nondancing members enjoying the balmy evening.
Ignoring their curious looks, Byron walked swiftly past
them, then down a path that led past the tennis courts to the
misty coolness of a small sunken garden surrounding a
modernistic fountain.

"Now no one can stare at us," he said, looking down at
Genie and at last releasing his hold on her.

"No," she agreed, although being alone with him in this
isolated spot made her feel even less comfortable. She still

had no idea why he had come tonight. It couldn't have been just to see her again, could it? Not after he had refused Mark's request so firmly.

"I can see a million questions in your mind," Byron said as if he could read hers. "Why don't you ask them?"

Disconcerted, Genie bit her lip and looked away. "I . . . I was wondering why you came tonight," she said. "Mark told me that you definitely wouldn't."

"Would you have stayed away if you'd known I was coming?" Byron asked.

"Oh, no!" Genie replied, raising her face and shaking her head quickly. Or would she? She wasn't sure. "I was just . . . surprised," she went on. "And glad, really. Mark did want to meet you. He's such a nice person."

"I liked him," Byron said. "Your sister's interesting, too. She seems to have a rather cosmic viewpoint about everything."

"Oh, she does," Genie said, feeling as if she must keep talking but hardly able to think straight. "She always looks for deep meanings in things, but she's really very sweet. What I mean is, she doesn't let that sort of thing interfere with her being a very kind and helpful person."

"She has nothing but good things to say about you, too," Byron said with a smile. "It's nice to meet two sisters who get along so well."

"We always have," Genie said.

"And your nephew, Tim, is their son?" Byron asked.

"That's right," Genie replied.

"He doesn't look much like either of them, with that black hair and those big dark eyes."

"He's adopted. He's of Mexican ancestry," Genie explained. "It's no secret. They knew he'd wonder about that, so they explained it to him when he was quite small."

Byron nodded. "That was wise of them. Children notice a lot more than most people give them credit for."

"They certainly do. Tim never misses anything. He even noticed that you looked like a pirate this morning."

"Did you think that I looked like a pirate?" Byron asked with an amused smile.

"Well, no. Actually I thought—" Genie stopped, blushing.

"I get the picture," Byron said, grinning at her discomfort. "I don't usually go out looking like that, but as I said this morning, I was in a hurry."

"Mmm-hmm," Genie murmured noncommittally. She was suddenly aware that they were talking about anything but the answer to her question. She frowned.

"More questions?" Byron asked.

"You didn't answer my first one," Genie said.

"Didn't I? Let's see. Why am I here. It's very simple. After I remembered where I'd seen your name, I called Mark to see if I was still invited tonight. I wanted to see you again."

"Oh." Genie frowned again. "I still don't understand. If you wanted to see me, all you had to do was stop at my house. I understood... that is, it was rumored that you avoided going out in public, especially to something like this party."

"I usually do," Byron replied gravely, "but I wanted to see what you'd be like at a party like this, and I also wanted to see how you'd react to my painting. I saw." He caught Genie's chin with his hand and raised her face to his, studying her intently. "I also wanted to see how I'd feel when I did. I'm still not sure."

"You're... you're not sure how you feel?" Genie stammered, staring into the dark depths of Byron's eyes, deep shadowed in the light filtering through the trees from the

perimeter lights high above them. She was only too sure
how she felt. Panicky. The desire to escape warred with
muscles that had lost their ability to move. Icy hot tingles
were running through her, and her knees were beginning to
feel wobbly again.

"No," Byron replied, "but I know how to find out." He
slid his hand behind Genie's waist and pulled her close to
him, his eyes never leaving hers until she was resting against
him. Then he slowly traced the curve of her lips with his
fingertip, following the movement with his eyes.

Genie held very still, scarcely breathing. She knew that
he was thinking of kissing her and found herself staring at
his mouth. The lower lip was full, the upper lip slightly
narrower and as gracefully curved as a woman's. Even
though he was not smiling, his mouth looked soft and in-
vitingly warm. The thought of that mouth touching her
own was both terribly frightening and at the same time un-
bearably alluring. How would she feel? She didn't think
that she was ready to find out, but, on the other hand, it
had been so long.... Numbly fascinated, she watched as
Byron's head bent toward her, his long hair falling forward across his cheeks. She shivered as his hand slipped
behind her neck.

The moment Byron's lips touched hers, the question was
answered in a dizzying flash of fire that shook Genie to her
toes. This couldn't be happening, she thought dimly, as her
hands crept upward. She clung to Byron's shoulders for
support, her fingers digging into the firm muscles. More
rockets went off as his tongue traced the line of her lips.
The tip of her tongue came out to meet his, and one hand
slid beneath his hair to curl around the warm, strong col-
umn of his neck. His tongue persisted, thrusting between
her lips, which parted to welcome his gentle invasion. A
shimmering brightness replaced the darkness around them

as desires she'd thought she might never feel again coursed through her, melting her fears away. Cradled in the haven of his strong arms, nestled against his hard body, Genie let out a long, shuddering sigh.

Byron responded with a soft, deep sound of pleasure. His hold tightened to an almost crushing strength, then relented, his hands moving eagerly over her back as if taking the measure of what he had found. His mouth found its way across her cheek and nuzzled beneath her ear. He caught her hair with one hand while the other slipped between them to caress her breasts. Through the thin fabric of her gown, his touch was electric. Soaring in a world of pure sensation, Genie pressed against him, suddenly wishing desperately that she had bought a less conservative dress. As if he had read her mind, Byron reached behind her and slid down the zipper and pushed her dress from one shoulder. He tantalized her with delicate pressure from his fingertips, then followed with a trail of deliciously soft kisses down her neck to find with his tongue the peaks that his fingers had raised to a fever pitch of ecstatic sensitivity. Genie plunged her hands deep into the thick, silky waves of his hair and groaned, her head flung back and her eyes closed. Rainbows of color flashed behind her closed lids, while storms of desire crashed within her. Byron let out a rasping moan and clutched her to him. She could feel his hardening pressure against her, and unconsciously she moved her hips in response. Then suddenly he stopped. He raised his head and roughly pushed her dress back onto her shoulder. Genie opened her eyes and stared wildly at him. Why did he look so angry?

He shook his head. "It won't work," he said, his voice low but harsh. "I can't let this happen." He caught Genie's face in his hand, his grip almost cruel. "I'm sorry, Genie," he said, his eyes profoundly sad as they held hers in their intense thrall. "It was my mistake." With that, he released her and turned and ran off back down the path.

CHAPTER TWO

STUNNED AT FIRST, Genie could only stand and stare after him. Then a wave of embarrassment washed through her, leaving her hot cheeked and trembling, tears pricking at her eyes. Good Lord, what had she been thinking of? Had she completely lost her mind? The way she had responded to Byron de Stefano, he must think . . .

With shaking fingers, Genie reached back and zipped up her dress, then started to walk slowly along the path toward the clubhouse, her shoulders hunched forward to shield the knot of misery that was lodged somewhere in her midsection. Conflicting thoughts tore through her mind. She never behaved like that. Never! No, be honest. With Kurt she had. But only when she knew they were going to be married. And she had never been that wild. It didn't feel the same. Not at all the same. What was different? Byron was attractive. Too attractive. He made her feel so alive. And confused. Completely confused. When he kissed her, she hardly knew what she was doing. Oh, come on. That was no excuse. Or was it? Maybe it wasn't Byron she had responded to at all. It couldn't be. She scarcely knew him. He reminded her of Kurt. In some ways. The long hair, about the same size and build. She missed Kurt. It had been so long. That must be it. She wanted, needed, someone to replace her lost love. Byron, too. Was that why he had stopped? Did she remind him of his late wife? Did he suddenly realize that she wasn't? Could never replace her? Or was it something simpler for him? Had he decided that he had misjudged her, and didn't want someone who appeared so easy to seduce? If he hadn't stopped when he did, she might have let him . . .

Genie stopped walking and clutched at the fence of the tennis court she was passing, feeling ill. She sank down onto one of the long benches beside the court and put her head in her hands. Tears trickled from her eyes, and her shoulders shook with silent sobs. She had been completely out of control. More than ever before in her entire life. She was so lonely. So terribly lonely.

"Are you all right, dear?" said a soft little voice.

Startled, Genie looked up just as Portia appeared like a muffin-shaped sprite and settled onto the bench beside her, sending a wave of her perfume wafting through the air. Portia put her arm around Genie's shoulders and handed her a dainty handkerchief from somewhere in her voluminous silver-and-gold gown.

"There, there," she said. "Go ahead and have a good cry, love. Everything will be all right. It's kismet, you know. I could feel it the minute I saw you and Byron together. When you were dancing, it was almost overwhelming. I saw you two leave together, and then I saw him come back by the clubhouse alone, looking upset. I don't know what happened, but never mind. That's not my affair."

Genie groaned and dabbed at a fresh shower of tears. Byron had looked upset. And she could tell by Portia's pregnant pause that she hoped Genie would tell her what happened. "He kissed me," she said, by way of partial explanation, knowing that Portia probably had guessed as much, anyway.

"And you slapped him?"

"No, but I should have," Genie said. She looked at her sister pleadingly. "I don't feel very well. I feel confused."

Portia gave Genie a sympathetic hug. "Of course you do. You liked it, didn't you? I think Byron's just as confused as you are, but don't worry. The cosmic spirits are at work, and it isn't always clear what their purpose is at first. You must wait and accept what they bring. But I think—" Portia's round cheeks dimpled with a smile "—in fact, after this morning I'm sure, that the celestial forces are right for something very good to happen for you, Genie. Something very good."

Genie shook her head and blew her nose. "I don't think so," she said glumly. "I think all your celestial forces are trying to tell me is that I'm supposed to spend the rest of my life a-alone." She stifled another sob and dabbed at her eyes.

"No," Portia said firmly, "that's not it at all. You've been shaken out of that stupor you've been in. You may not like it, but it's good for you."

"You're right, I don't like it," Genie grumbled. "I think I'll go on home now. I don't feel much like partying anymore tonight."

"You'll do no such thing," Portia said. "You'll repair your makeup and come back to the party. You'll feel much better if you do." At Genie's defiant look, she added, "You don't want everyone to think that you ran off with Byron de Stefano, do you? That would really give the gossips something to talk about." She smiled mischievously. "I might even tell them that you did."

Genie glared at her. "Why do you have to suddenly turn mean on me?" she asked. "I've had a long hard day and I'm tired."

"I'm not being mean, I'm trying to protect you so the celestial forces can do their work without interference from a lot of ridiculous humans," Portia said. "Come along, now." She took Genie's arm and gently started her off toward the clubhouse.

With a sigh, Genie went along. Portia was probably right, at least about the gossips. Not only that, but she wouldn't want the young men of the club to think that all they had to do to win her favors was to let their hair grow and wear tight black leather pants. The thought of an epidemic of that style sweeping the conservative young executives at the Heavenly Valley Tennis Club made her smile to herself even through her gloom. It would be utterly ridiculous. Besides, none of them could begin to look the way Byron de Stefano did.

Genie repaired her makeup under Portia's close scrutiny, then accompanied her back to the party, under strict orders to smile her head off and dance with anyone who asked her.

"Why is it the cosmic forces can't take care of things if I don't smile and dance?" Genie complained.

"Oh, they'll take care of things," Portia said seriously, "but you might not like it if they turn against you. You have to be ready for their help."

"I'm ready, believe me," Genie said grimly. She told herself that she didn't really believe in Portia's mystical forces, but when they neared the dining room, she counted to ten and pasted a smile on her face, reasoning that a sour face would also give the gossipy tongues plenty to wag about. She had no sooner entered the room than Bob Welch invited her to dance. With an even brighter smile, she accepted, and for the next hour found herself circling the floor with one man after another. It was, she discovered, almost fun, except that none of them danced as well as Byron. But then, she was unlikely to have that experience again.

By eleven o'clock, Genie's feet were protesting against the high heels she wore. Even Portia did not object when she pleaded exhaustion and said she was going home.

"Aren't you glad you stayed?" Portia asked, with an I-told-you-so look.

"I think I will be when my feet recover," Genie replied. She went to the locker room and changed into her warm-up suit and sandals, then drove away from the club with a sigh of relief. She had managed to escape the party without making any commitments to future engagements, but she could tell that Bob Welch had been encouraged enough to persist. He was, she mused as she drove along, the nicest of the lot. Maybe, if she got her courage up, she'd go out with him sometime soon. Even if she could never be serious about him, it would be better than sitting home alone night after night. It didn't take any cosmic influences to tell her that. Good, practical common sense told her that she didn't want to spend the rest of her life as a hermit. It made people weird. Being alone too much was probably the reason she had so completely lost her head when Byron kissed her. Yes, she definitely needed to get out more. Portia had been right about her going back to the party. She did feel much better now.

Genie parked in the carport and went to get her suitcase from the trunk, her mouth twisting in a wry smile as she looked at her damaged fender glistening in the moonlight. Kismet? She shook her head. She had probably just not been alert enough. Still, her family had been backing out of that driveway for more than twenty years without getting hit. And she really hadn't seen any sign of Byron de Stefano's car in the distance....

She went through the door at the back of the carport, mounted the steps to the deck, then let out a stifled scream as a dark figure suddenly rose from the lounge chair.

"My God, what are you doing here?" she cried, recognizing almost instantly the form of Byron de Stefano, dressed in a dark-colored sweat suit. "You scared me half to death!"

"I'm sorry. I went out for a jog. I wanted to talk to you so I came back here to wait. I sat down on the lounge, but it was so comfortable that I guess I dozed off." His white teeth flashed in a grin in the dim light. "That sounds like Goldilocks and the Three Bears, doesn't it?"

"Sort of," Genie agreed, although she felt more like Little Red Riding Hood confronting the wolf. Had Byron decided that he wanted to follow through with a woman who had acted as if she was only too ready to hop into bed with him? She took a step backward as he advanced toward her. "What did you want to talk about?" she asked warily.

"I thought I should explain why I said what I did earlier," Byron replied. "I was afraid I sounded like some kind of a mental case." As Genie sidled toward the door to the house he added, "Don't be frightened. I'm not crazy, and I didn't come here to attack you. May I come in for a few minutes? I won't keep you long. I know you must be tired."

"I—I guess so," Genie said. The idea of letting him into her house made her anxious, but Byron sounded different now, almost painfully polite, as if he had been as embarrassed as she was, and while she still felt embarrassed about her earlier behavior, she was even more curious about what he might have to say.

She unlocked the sliding door and reached inside for the light switch. "Come on in," she invited him. "Oops! Watch the cats." Ms. Kitty had appeared from nowhere and shot through the opening as soon as the light came on.

"Well, look at that," Byron said, smiling at the sight of the kittens following moments later in single file, their tails stuck straight up in the air. He bent and picked up the last one, a tiny calico, and carried it inside. "Are you going to be giving these away?" he asked, caressing the kitten with one long finger and then rubbing his cheek against it.

"In about a week," Genie answered, feeling her tension begin to ebb at the sight of the overwhelmingly masculine Byron de Stefano so obviously completely won over by a tiny ball of fluff that scarcely covered the palm of his hand. "Can I pawn one off on you?" she asked, smiling when he scrunched up one eye while the kitten licked his cheek with its minuscule rough tongue.

"This one," he replied without hesitation. "I love its colors."

"I'm afraid *it* is sure to be a female," Genie warned. "Calicos always are."

"That's all right," Byron said. "If the population increases too much I'll have her spayed."

Genie nodded. "I should have Ms. Kitty done, now that she's had a batch of kittens." As she went to the refrigerator, she waved in the direction of the table that sat in front of the glass wall overlooking the deck. "Sit down. Would you like a Coke or something?"

"Sure. Thanks," Byron replied. He sat at the table, the kitten still in his hands. "Did you say this was your parents' house?"

"It still is," Genie said as she got out a tray of ice cubes and a couple of glasses. "I'm house-sitting while they're in England. My father's on sabbatical from the university. I usually live a lot closer to the club." She poured the Coke, waiting for the fizz to die down so that she could fill the glasses.

"But you lived here most of your life?"

"Yes. When my parents built this house it was the last one on the road. They couldn't afford the prices up here nowadays."

"Then it turned out to be a good investment."

"Yes, it certainly did."

Genie carried the glasses to the table, suddenly aware, as Byron looked up and smiled at her, that they had been conversing as casually as if nothing at all had happened between them earlier. Which was, she thought as she felt her nerves tighten, exactly the way she wanted to keep it. She sat down and took a swallow of her drink.

"How long have you lived up here?" she asked.

"About four years," Byron replied. "I lived in New York City before that." His expression darkened and he looked down at the kitten. "Which brings me indirectly to what I wanted to tell you." He sighed and put the kitten on the floor, then looked back at Genie. "This isn't an easy thing to talk about, but I don't know any way except to be direct."

He paused and studied Genie's face, his own face lined with tension. It was, she thought, a very different expression than she had seen on his face before. He looked both worried and unhappy and, instead of being uncomfortable under his scrutiny, she felt a sympathetic tug of unhappiness in her own heart.

"Go ahead," she encouraged him.

Byron smiled crookedly. "All right. You see, five years ago last September my wife and baby son were killed in that earthquake that hit Mexico City."

Genie nodded, but said nothing. There was, she knew only too well, nothing that anyone could say to assuage that kind of grief.

"I fell apart pretty badly after that," Byron went on in a low voice. "It was bad enough burying my wife, but almost worse was the fact that no trace was ever found of my—" his voice cracked and he cleared his throat "—of my son. He'd have been about the age of your nephew by now. I'm always reminded when I see a boy that age, especially one of Mexican ancestry. My...my wife was Mexican." He took a deep breath and shook his head. "Anyway, after about a year had passed, I decided to move West to get away from all the familiar things, hoping that I'd learn to live with what had happened and be able to get on with my work. As far as my work goes, I've been successful, but—"

Byron stopped and ran his fingers nervously through his hair, then tossed his head back and smiled wryly at Genie. "I'm probably not making much sense to you. What I'm trying to say is that I'm still not over what happened, and maybe I never will be. I find you very attractive, which I suppose was obvious to you earlier. Too attractive, I'm afraid. It brings back all of the old fears of finding someone only to lose them again. I can't work when I get in that state, and without my work I'm nothing. Which is why I ran away, and why I won't be asking you out like any normal man who's just met an attractive woman." He paused again and studied Genie's face intently for several seconds. "Now you probably do think I'm a mental case," he said finally.

"No, not at all," Genie said softly. She knew only too well how he felt. She thought of telling him about Kurt, but decided against it. That was her problem to solve, and Byron had enough to bear. "I do hope that you recover someday," she went on slowly, "but I'm glad that you can keep on with your work in the meantime. I—I'm afraid I didn't adequately convey to you this evening how much your painting impressed me. I don't think I know the words to do so."

To Genie's surprise, Byron muttered an expletive and then buried his face in his hands. When he looked up again, his eyes were misty. "I'll always treasure your compliment," he said huskily. "Thank you." He pushed his chair back and stood up. "I'd better be going. It's a long way back to my house, and uphill all the way."

"I'll turn on the outside lights," Genie said, rising and following him to the door.

"Don't bother. I can see well enough," Byron said. He stopped partway through the door and looked down at Genie. "Why haven't you married yet?" he asked, frowning at her almost accusingly.

Startled, Genie stared at him blankly for a moment, fighting an impulse to tell him that she was just as frightened as he was. "I don't know. Just never met the right man, I guess," she replied, trying to keep her voice light.

Byron's eyes narrowed. He scanned Genie's face intently, and she could see a million thoughts racing through his mind within the dark depths of his eyes. "Afraid of making a commitment, like so many people seem to be these days?" he asked finally.

"No," Genie replied honestly. That was not what she feared.

"You're afraid of something," Byron said, still frowning. "I can see it in your eyes."

Genie felt her throat tighten uncomfortably. He was too perceptive. "I'm just tired," she said, trying to smile. "It's been a long day."

"And it didn't start out too well," Byron said, returning a crooked smile. "Well, good night."

"Good night."

Byron at last stepped out onto the deck. Genie put her hand on the door to slide it closed behind him, but something stopped her. It would be so final, closing that door

behind him. The thought made the tight ache in her throat
return. Instead, she followed him outside and stood in the
middle of the deck, her hands thrust deep in her pockets,
watching as he went to the stairs. He paused, his hand on
the railing, and looked back, then up at the misty moon
hovering in the west.

"Beautiful night," he said.

"Yes, it is," Genie agreed. She looked toward the moon,
then at the stars overhead. Suddenly she let out a little gasp
at the sight of a shooting star darting across the sky, leaving a brilliant trail behind it. "Did you see that?" she
whispered, turning her eyes toward Byron as an involuntary shiver went through her.

"A lovely sight," Byron said, his voice low and husky.

Their eyes met and held in spite of the darkness, and for
a moment Genie had the incredible impression that the
phosphorescent brightness of the meteorite's trail was filling the space between them.

"Genie, would you do something for me?" Byron said
at last.

"What?"

"Go back into the house and close the door and lock it."

The softness had left Byron's voice. It was harsh with
strain. Genie understood. Wordlessly, she turned and did
as he asked. She turned off the lights, tears pricking at her
eyes. Through the darkened house she moved to stand and
watch out the front window of her room as Byron appeared on the road at the top of the driveway and turned to
go toward his home. He took a few steps, stopped and
looked back at the house. For a long time he stood there,
motionless. Then he put his head down and started up the
hill. In only seconds he was gone from view.

Genie sank down onto her bed and stared numbly into
the darkness before her, while tears ran unchecked down

her cheeks. The desolate feeling of loneliness she felt earlier had returned, much worse than before. She felt as if all hope of sunshine, light and laughter had gone out of her life forever. Without even undressing, she curled up on her bed and pulled the comforter over her, wishing miserably that she could forget this day had ever happened. Like the flash of a shooting star, Byron de Stefano had come rocketing into her life and then vanished into the darkness, touching her briefly and then pulling away. Too afraid. They were both too afraid. With a sob, Genie buried her face in the pillow. She couldn't think about it. It was too hard. In seconds she was asleep.

CHAPTER THREE

THE BELL was ringing so close to her ear that it felt like sandpaper. Genie brushed at it impatiently. Good Lord, it was the cat! And the telephone. She turned over and flung her hand toward the phone.

"Yowr!" said Ms. Kitty from beneath her.

"Oh God. Sorry," Genie said, suddenly coming awake. She thrust herself off the cat and grabbed the telephone. "H'lo?"

"Where on earth were you? Out in the back forty?" said a perky, lilting voice.

"No, I was asleep," Genie replied, recognizing the voice of her old friend Sondra Parks.

"Asleep? It's after ten o'clock. What happened? Did you stay up reading a good book?"

Genie groaned and sat up. Last night. Yesterday. Byron. Had it all really happened? The ache inside told her that it had. She groaned again.

"Genie? What's wrong? Are you sick?" Sondra sounded worried.

"No, just . . . there was a big party at the club last night. I—I think I overdid it a little," Genie replied. And she had kissed Byron de Stefano, and come home to find him waiting. . . .

"You drank too much?" Sondra now sounded incredulous.

"No, of course not. I can't explain. Something happened, and I... Oh, it's just too complicated. I'm all right." Except that she felt like a cold, leaden weight had moved in where her heart used to be, a sensation even worse than the numbness that had followed Kurt's death.

"You don't sound all right," Sondra said. "Do you want to talk about it?"

"I don't know," Genie said with a heavy sigh. Sondra was smart and sensible, a successful businesswoman, not given to flights of fancy like Portia. Maybe it would help. And then again, nothing would.

"Why don't you come on down for brunch?" Sondra suggested. "I've got some beautiful mangos and fresh pineapple, and I'll fix you some of those Swedish pancakes you love."

After a few moments' thought, Genie agreed. Ordinarily, being home alone on Sunday was a treat she looked forward to. Today the idea had no appeal at all. "Don't go overboard," she warned. "I'm not very hungry."

"You'd better be ready to tell me what's wrong," Sondra said firmly. "You sound perfectly awful."

"Thanks. I feel awful," Genie replied. "See you in a while."

She dragged herself out of bed, took a shower and put on jeans and a red sweatshirt, fed the cat and then shooed her and the kittens out the door, all without looking once at the table where Byron de Stefano had sat. Then she picked up her purse and went out the front door, avoiding the deck, avoiding looking at the place at the top of the driveway where he had stood. When she tried to put the key into her car's ignition, her hand shook so that it took several attempts.

"Oh, stop it!" she said aloud, banging her fist against her forehead, suddenly angry with herself. She was acting like an idiot! As if in one day Byron de Stefano had cast some kind of magical spell over her. She had been listening to Portia and her mystical portents too much lately. No more of that nonsense. "No more, do you hear?" she muttered, setting her jaw and backing carefully out of the driveway.

It was only a short drive to the quaint miniature mall near the beach where Sondra lived in an apartment over her arts-and-crafts shop. On the way, Genie resolved not to burden Sondra with her problem. It would pass. She would be fine in a day or two. She parked behind the shop and climbed the steep stairs to the little balcony where Sondra grew an amazing assortment of herbs in neat rows of red clay pots. Sondra, Genie thought, pausing to admire them, was so organized.

"Oh, there you are," Sondra's voice came from the doorway. "I thought I heard footsteps on the stairs."

"Your herbs look so beautiful I had to admire them," Genie said, smiling at her friend. "I'd try to grow some on the deck if I thought they'd survive my brown thumb."

"I can show you the easiest ones after we eat," Sondra offered. "Come on in. I'm starved, even if you're not."

"You don't look like you're starved," Genie teased. Sondra's perennial battle with extra weight while Genie remained thin had always been a source of friendly needling between them.

Sondra grimaced and shook her head, her long dark ponytail swishing back and forth on her shoulders. "And I never will," she said with a sigh. "Sit down while I finish the bacon."

The balcony door opened into Sondra's tidy little kitchen, another masterpiece, Genie thought, of her artistic and organizational abilities. Rows of neatly labeled jars and canisters stood on brightly painted shelves done in rainbow hues. The cabinets were painted a creamy white, the countertops covered in a yellow linen-patterned Formica. A little round table wore a bright yellow cloth with a bouquet of silk daisies in a jade-green pot in the middle. Two sparkling glass bowls of colorful fruit were already set on the table.

"That fruit looks beautiful," Genie said as she took a seat. "I think I'm hungry, after all."

"Eat up. There's more," Sondra said. She lifted several strips of bacon from an iron frying pan onto a paper towel and then sat down opposite Genie. "Now," she said, propping her elbows on the table and scrutinizing Genie seriously, "tell me what's bothering you."

Genie popped a large piece of pineapple into her mouth and shook her head. "Nothing serious," she mumbled. "Eat your fruit."

"Nothing serious? You look like death warmed over," Sondra replied. "Pale. Circles under your eyes. Come on. I'm not blind."

"No, really. Nothing I can't deal with," Genie said. "I'd rather talk about something interesting. What's the latest hot item in the arts-and-crafts business?"

"Mmm. Let me show you," Sondra said, her face suddenly becoming animated. "Come into the living room a minute."

"Yes, ma'am," Genie said, smiling as she got up and followed Sondra. Sondra's enthusiasm for her business was still as infectious as when she had started several years before.

"There," Sondra said, making an expansive gesture toward a striking colorful print on the wall above her sofa. "Isn't it beautiful? You know whose work it is, don't you?"

Genie stared at the print, her throat tight, her earlier resolve crumbling to ashes. The rhythmic patterns, the bold colors, evoking dolphins at play in the sea were unmistakably the work of Byron de Stefano. "De Stefano," she whispered.

"Yes. Isn't it marvelous? He's agreed to let me market a whole set of signed and numbered prints," Sondra said. "It's the first time—" She stopped and looked at Genie, who was standing with her eyes closed, tears running down her cheeks. "Good heavens, what's wrong? You *are* sick! Come and lie down on the sofa."

"No!" Genie ran back into the kitchen and sat down. She picked up her napkin and angrily rubbed the tears from her cheeks. "All right, I'll tell you what's wrong," she said harshly, "only you're going to think I've lost my mind."

"No, I won't," Sondra said softly. "We're old friends, remember? Come on, now, start at the beginning."

Genie nodded. "It's not a very long story," she said with a rueful smile. "It all happened yesterday." She went through the events of the previous day, from the rumpled fender to Byron de Stefano's exit into the night. "And that's all of it," she said in conclusion. "Now you tell me. Why do I feel so miserable? Is it because he makes me think of Kurt and miss him all over again?"

Sondra shook her head. "If I thought that was it, I *would* think there's something wrong with you. No, my friend, you're in love with Byron. It happens that way sometimes, like a bolt from the blue. Maybe it's fate, or—"

"Stop that! You sound just like Portia," Genie grumbled. "I don't believe in love at first sight, or any of that other nonsense, either."

Sondra shrugged. "Believe what you want to. You asked me why you feel miserable, and it's the only logical reason

I can think of. Either that or you've got some strange new virus."

"Maybe that's it, but what difference does it make? He's gone. He won't be back. Period. Finis."

"Nonsense. He'll be back. He has to talk himself into it, but he will. That episode last night wouldn't have happened if he wasn't halfway convinced he should already."

Genie gave a short, dry laugh. "A lot of good it will do if he does come back. We're both so scared that we'll lose someone again that we're afraid to get close to anyone new. Some romance that would be."

"Oh, for heaven's sake," Sondra said in exasperated tones, "do you intend to let that ruin the rest of your life? There's risk involved in everything. You have to face it and go ahead, anyway. Good Lord, Genie, Byron de Stefano's worth it! If it weren't for Sam, I'd throw myself at him like a ton of bricks."

"Don't do that," Genie said with a smile. "Byron would probably never be able to paint again." Sondra's fiancé, Sam, was a huge, muscular physical-education teacher who kept a very jealous eye on his love.

"Don't worry," Sondra said, "I won't try to muscle in on your territory. Now, how about some pancakes to digest along with all of the words of wisdom I've given you?"

"I'm ready for the pancakes," Genie said with a sigh. "As for the wisdom, I guess I hope you're right that he'll be back, but I'm not even sure of that. Sometimes I really wish there was something to all of those premonitions and prognostications of Portia's. Then I could just relax and let it all happen."

Sondra raised her eyebrows and gave Genie a wry smile. "And just what else do you think you can do?" she asked.

For days afterward, that statement of Sondra's stayed in Genie's mind more than any other. There was, after all, nothing she could do to change the future. Byron either would come back, or he wouldn't. They would either get over their mutual anxieties, or they wouldn't. In the meantime...

"You look cross as a bear," Portia said, meeting Genie outside her court as she came to pick up Tim after his session with Genie's children's class on the following Friday morning. "The little darlings give you a hard time today?"

"I'm just hot and tired," Genie said, shaking her head. "It's been a long week." And there had been no sign of Byron de Stefano. Trying to convince herself to accept whatever happened had done little good. Day by day she grew more tense. Even physically exhausted, she was having trouble sleeping.

"No word from Byron?" Portia asked. She smiled as Genie frowned. "Aha! So that's it."

"It is not," Genie denied, resenting Portia's ability to zero in on her problem as if she could read her mind. She had not even told Portia about Byron's return the night of the club party.

Portia ignored her denial. "Don't fret so," she said, patting Genie's arm. "Even with cosmic help, these things take time. There have to be valleys before you ascend the peaks."

"Some cosmic help," Genie said, toweling her dripping face and arms. "I think they're turning this into Death Valley. Let's go and have a Coke."

"Don't scoff," Portia said, floating along at Genie's side as they walked toward the shaded terrace. "There was a sure sign last Saturday. A really spectacular shooting star. And on the night that you two met. Did you see it? It was beautiful."

Why deny that? Genie thought with a sigh. "Yes, I saw it. I was out on the deck."

"Wonderful!" Portia said happily. "Now, if I just knew whether Byron saw it, too, I could not only say that you two belong together, but that you'll definitely be married within the year."

Genie stopped dead in her tracks. "Portia," she said plaintively, "why do you say things like that? It was just a meteorite that got caught in the earth's gravitational field. It doesn't mean anything for human beings unless they happen to get hit by one."

"Nonsense," Portia replied. "People have been documenting such things since the beginning of time."

"Oh, sure," Genie said sarcastically. "Really scientific. Even Peter Pan had it figured out."

"You'll see," Portia said, undaunted. "You'll see."

The trouble was, Genie thought that evening as she stretched out on the lounge on the deck and watched the stars come out one by one, that people wanted so desperately to believe in magical portents. In spite of everything she knew, she couldn't help thinking of Portia's starry prediction, and wondering if there might be something to it. She fondled Byron's kitten, lying curled up on her chest, then picked it up and rubbed her cheek against it. It was a tiny miracle, she thought. Why not believe in others? She put it down again and closed her tired eyes. Why not? she thought, and drifted off to sleep.

A cool, damp breeze awakened her. She opened her eyes. It was pitch-dark, clouds now obscuring the stars. *Better go inside before I catch a cold,* she thought sleepily, pushing herself to a sitting position. She swung her feet to the deck and looked around for the kittens. Out of the corner of her eye, she saw something bright and turned her head.

"My God!" she gasped, recognizing the glowing end of a cigarette and behind it, the familiar shape of Byron de Stefano's dark mane of hair. "Do you always have to startle me like that?" she complained, as her heart began to race.

"I'm sorry," he said. "You looked so comfortable that I hesitated to wake you. I would have soon, though. It's getting chilly."

"Yes, it is," Genie agreed, rubbing her bare arms vigorously, although she was no longer feeling cold at all. Inside, she felt as if an electric current had been turned on. "Do you want to come in?" she asked, getting shakily to her feet.

"Yes. I wanted to try talking to you again. It didn't seem to work the last time." He got up and followed her to the door.

"Oh?" Genie looked up at him questioningly, able to see his face as the light came on. "Wait," she said, holding her arm in front of him.

"There they are." Byron smiled as Ms. Kitty and her family paraded through the opening. "How's my little gal doing?"

"Just fine. I've started them on milk and kitty food. You could probably take her home with you if you want to." Genie watched as Byron picked up the calico kitten and tickled its chin with his forefinger. She didn't really want him to take the kitten yet. If he did, there would be no reminder of him in her house anymore. If he went away again.

"I think I'll wait a little longer, if you don't mind," Byron said, putting the kitten down again. "She may still need her mommy."

"No problem," Genie said, feeling relieved. Perhaps Byron, too, wanted to keep that connection. And cats had often been given credit for having magical powers. At that thought, Genie grimaced to herself. She was getting more like Portia all the time. "Would you like a Coke, or something warm, like coffee or tea?" she asked. She saw Byron looking around for an ashtray and handed him one from the shelf on the low dividing wall that separated the kitchen from the dining area.

"Thanks," he said, stubbing out his cigarette. "I didn't want to start smoking again, but something drove me to it this past week. I can't seem to get a damn thing done."

"I'm used to smokers," Genie said. "My father's tried to quit several times, but he claims he can't think at all when he does."

"I quit for several years," Byron said, coming to lean on the dividing wall as Genie went into the kitchen. "It's your fault I've started again." There was a wry half smile on his face.

"My fault?" Genie raised her eyebrows at him, then looked away from the disturbing glimmer in his eyes. "Coffee?"

"Fine. I'm afraid I didn't do a very good job of convincing myself that I didn't want to see you again. And I kept seeing the hurt look on your face when I told you to go inside."

Genie cast him a sideways glance as she measured out the coffee. "Blame me if you want to," she said with a shrug, "but I don't remember handing you a single cigarette."

"I know. It's a lousy excuse," Byron replied.

He sounded gruff. Genie set the coffeepot on and looked over at him and smiled. He looked as out of sorts as she had felt all week. His hair was tousled, and the collar of his shirt was only partway out of the neck of the dark blue sweater he had pulled on over it. She longed to go to him and fix the collar and smooth his hair back from his forehead. Instead she said, "Shall we sit down while the coffee brews? My feet are still tired from being on them all week."

"I don't know how you do it," Byron said, his eyes on Genie as he moved toward the table and she came around the end of the wall. "At least it keeps you fit."

"Yes, you can say that much for it," she said, waiting until he had taken a seat before she sat down. She felt safer with some space between them. The air seemed charged with tension, as if they were both thinking and feeling much more than their polite conversation indicated. Byron was looking at her thoughtfully. She returned his gaze for a moment, then dropped her eyes and began fiddling with the fringed edge of the red-checked place mat on the table in front of her. If he had come to talk, let him start the conversation. She couldn't think of a single sensible thing to say.

"I don't think we got enough out in the open last time," he said at last.

"About what?" Genie returned, lifting her eyes again.

"About you," Byron replied. "Some things told me you were a beautiful, passionate, carefree young woman. Your eyes told me differently. I should have believed your eyes."

Genie frowned. "I don't know what you're talking about."

"Yes, you do. I was talking to your sister—"

"You were doing what?!" Genie interrupted, her frown turning to a glare. "What do you mean, snooping around behind my back and—"

"Calm down. I wasn't snooping. Portia called to invite me to a party. She wants me to bring you. When I, uh, expressed some reservations she told me that she's been worried about you for some time. She told me what happened to your fiancé."

"She had no right," Genie fumed, getting up and going back to the kitchen. So much for Portia's reliance on cosmic forces, she thought bitterly. Or did she have some notion that she had been anointed as their messenger? She jerked open the cupboard and took out two mugs, almost bumping into Byron as she turned to carry them to the counter by the coffeepot.

"Why didn't you tell me?" Byron asked, taking the cups from her and setting them on the counter. "God knows, I'd understand how you feel."

"Because it's *my* problem," Genie said, removing the pot from its stand with a shaky hand.

"Here, let me do that," Byron said. He steered her hand back to place the pot down again, then took it himself and filled the cups. "I'm not sure it is just your problem anymore," he said as he carried the cups back to the table.

"I don't see why not," Genie said testily. "Mine is mine and yours is yours."

"And never the twain shall meet?" Byron asked, a gentle twinkle in his eyes.

Genie looked at him over the rim of her cup and smiled in spite of herself. There was something so solid and strong-looking about him. It was hard to believe he was afraid of anything.

"That's better," he said. He took a swallow of his coffee and then leaned forward, his face more serious. "Genie," he said, "I don't want to invade your privacy, but I thought it might help both of us if we talk about our problems. Lord knows, I don't want to spend the rest of my life a prisoner of the past."

"I don't, either," Genie said with a sigh. "I keep making resolutions to try and change, but it doesn't seem to help."

"I know how that goes," Byron said with feeling. "I've gone out to have a good time, as if it were all behind me, and ended up feeling completely alone in the midst of a hundred people. Like part of me is missing."

"Oh, Byron," Genie said sympathetically, her heart touched by the anguish she could read in his eyes. "You must have loved your wife very much. Do you . . . do you want to tell me about her?"

Byron looked down and chewed his lip, his forehead furrowed in anxious lines. "I don't know. I've never done that. Could you tell me about . . . was his name Kurt?"

"Yes, his name was Kurt." Genie took a deep breath. Could she? It made her feel uncomfortable to think of telling Byron about Kurt, as if she would be saying, This is what the man I loved was like, and no one can take his place. But that was not the way she felt, not really. When she looked into Byron's tortured eyes, all that she felt was a longing to help him. Would it help Byron talk out his fears if she could do it? Would it help her? So far, nothing else had. It was worth a try.

"He was a marine biologist," she began slowly. "We met the summer I decided I couldn't really make it on the pro tour. I was feeling pretty down . . ."

Genie went on to describe the two years she had known Kurt, how he had made her feel happy again, the plans they had made. It didn't hurt as much as she had thought it would to talk about him. But when it came to telling how she had felt when her father had broken the news to her of Kurt's death she stopped, dashing the tears from her cheeks. "I think you know that part," she said hoarsely.

"I do indeed," Byron said, his own voice husky with emotion.

"More coffee?" Genie said, getting up and going to the kitchen without waiting for a reply. The gentle understanding on Byron's face was threatening to bring on a flood of tears. She had just taken hold of the coffeepot when she felt Byron's hands on her shoulders. "D-don't," she said, holding herself rigid. There was nothing in the world that she would like more than to feel his arms around her, but she did not want his pity.

Byron's hands tightened on her shoulders, and he bent his head to lay his cheek against hers. "I only wanted to thank you," he said softly. He moved away and Genie turned toward him.

"Your turn," she said.

At first he looked as if he was going to refuse, then he lifted his chin and nodded. "All right," he said. He sat down and watched as Genie refilled their cups and then returned to sit opposite him. For a long time he said nothing. Then he began.

"My story's a little longer," he said, staring into his coffee cup as if he could see it pictured in the rising steam. "My wife, Consuela, was a native of Mexico, but she came to this country for musical training at the Juilliard School in New York. She was a pianist. A beautiful girl, with ebony hair and huge dark eyes. One look, and I fell in love with her. But I was a struggling artist then, and she came from a wealthy family. In spite of our differences, we found that we had a great deal in common. Before long we decided to get married. It took over a year to convince her family that I would be a suitable husband, but we finally managed it when I had my first one-man show at a well-known gallery. For two years we were very happy, both of us advancing in our work. We hadn't planned on children, but we were very happy when Connie found out that she was pregnant."

Byron paused and smiled wryly. "I still don't know whether she forgot her birth control pills deliberately or not. Anyway, little Tony was born in May of 1985. Connie's family wanted to see him and have him baptized in their church in Oaxaca, so we flew down as soon as our schedules permitted. In September. We spent a week there and then flew on to Mexico City, where I had some business to attend to. We were staying in a fine hotel. The kind that looks as if it's been around forever. I'd gone out for a jog early in the morning while Connie tended to getting the baby fed and ready for the day. I was heading back toward the hotel when I noticed the ground beginning to tremble under my feet. For a second I didn't know what was happening. . . ."

He paused again and took a deep breath before going on, "Then there was an awful roaring sound, as everything around me began to move in rhythm with the earth. Pieces of buildings began to fall into the street nearby, crashing like thunder. I stopped. I could see the hotel shuddering like a giant hand was shaking it. Every instinct in me told me to run, but I stood there, staring at it as it began to crumble, knowing that I was watching something terrible, knowing that my wife and child were in there and—" Byron buried his face in his hands, his shoulders shaking "—and there was nothing I could do," he finished in a hoarse whisper.

Genie watched helplessly as he tried to control himself, fighting back tears of her own. Dear God, how could he bear it? If she had been there when Kurt died, watching, unable to do anything to help. . . .

At last Byron raised his head, his eyes still swimming with tears. "I still can't believe it," he said. "Not so much that they're dead, but the way it happened. The power of that earthquake. It's unimaginable. They give it numbers on a scale, but it doesn't tell the story. Watching a city fall before your eyes. I still have nightmares about it. And then the screaming of the ambulances, the frantic cries of the trapped and broken people. God knows how I escaped with only a broken nose from some falling debris. I stayed and helped for days with the rescue effort, praying until the last that Connie and Tony would be found in one of those miraculous little spaces that saved some people, but they weren't. Connie had been crushed like a flower ground under some giant's heel. Tony... I guess I'll never know. We never found him. He was so... so tiny." Tears ran unchecked now down Byron's cheeks as he sat and stared at Genie. "I don't know, Genie," he said at last. "Will I ever be able to forget?"

"Forget?" Genie shook her head. "I don't think so. Some things are beyond forgetting." It was not, she thought sadly, what she would have liked to say to the handsome man who sat across from her, his face drawn and sad from the memories he had endured once again, but she knew it was true. There was no forgetting an experience like that. "All you can do," she said softly, "is learn not to look back too often. I guess that when you're painting, you're able to do that. Your pictures don't look sad."

"That's true." Byron stood up abruptly and went to fill his mug again. "Now I won't sleep for a week," he said dryly, taking a long drink and then setting the mug on the dividing wall and leaning on his elbows beside it. "You know what bothers me almost more than the fact that my memories haunt me?" he said, his voice returning to a more conversational tone. "It's the fact that I know other people have gone through worse times and managed to get on with their lives. My father was in the infantry in World War II. His unit helped liberate a concentration camp. My God. What those people endured. And yet, some of them survived and carried on. It makes me feel like... like an inadequate fool."

"An inadequate fool? With your talent? Don't be ridiculous?" Genie scolded. "It's not as if you'd spent the past five years doing nothing but whining and complaining. You paint a world that's beautiful and alive. Somewhere deep inside you must feel that way."

"Deep inside? It's not buried at all, most of the time. I love life. It's a beautiful world. I thought I had things under control until I met you." He pulled a cigarette from his pocket and lit it. "See what you've done to me?" he said with a teasing smile.

"You haven't helped me a lot, either," Genie said, giving him a cold look. "But I'm not about to start smoking. I'll just keep on staying home alone with my cats until I'm an ugly old woman."

"No, you won't. I won't let you." Byron crushed out his cigarette angrily, then ran his fingers through his hair, his eyes bright and intense as he looked over at Genie.

"I don't think it's up to you," she replied, lifting her chin defiantly. That masterful gleam in Byron's eyes had set off a warning shock within her that was far harder for her to cope with than his unhappy memories.

"Oh, yes it is." Byron came swiftly around the dividing wall, took hold of Genie's hand and pulled her to her feet. "This is what it all comes down to," he said, taking her face in his hand and tilting it toward him. "We can talk until we're blue in the face, and we understand each other's past like few other people could do, but when we get beyond that to where we begin to feel something new—" he lowered his face until his mouth was only a breath away from Genie's "—that's when it all falls apart, and we run away," he whispered. "And we're not going to keep doing that."

Genie stood perfectly still, her heart beating like a triphammer. Byron's face was so close that all she could see was the deep dark centers of his eyes. She could feel his breath on her lips, the soft brush of his hair against her cheeks. Run away? She couldn't run if she wanted to. But he didn't mean to actually run. She knew that. He meant that they were still afraid. Was he right? Could they stop being afraid? Was he going to kiss her now and start to teach her that she shouldn't be frightened? Having him so close was making it hard for her to breath. Staring into his eyes was making her dizzy. His eyes were such deep endless pools. She could feel herself falling...

"Good Lord, Genie," Byron said, his arms closing around her, "are you that frightened?"

"No," Genie whispered, clinging to him for support as the room reeled around her. "I think I'm just tired. I'd...better go to bed."

Byron swore softly and lifted her into his arms. "No wonder you're exhausted. It's almost four in the morning. I've kept you up all night. Which way is your room?"

"The...front of the house, on the right," Genie said, closing her eyes and nestling her head against Byron's chest. It felt so good. He was so warm and strong. "Don't want to go to bed," she mumbled. "Not afraid. I want you...to hold me." She could feel Byron's muscles tighten.

"I want to hold you, my sweet," he murmured against her hair, "but I don't think I'd better. Maybe sometime soon." He found the light switch and carried Genie to her bed. "There you are," he said, setting her carefully down on the edge of the bed. "Will you be all right now?"

"I think so." Genie nodded. "Thanks. I don't usually get dizzy like...like some silly Victorian."

Byron smiled. "I know. You're worn out. Do you have to teach in the...later this morning?"

"At nine o'clock," Genie said with a sigh.

"Can I call someone for you and tell them to cancel your lessons until noon?"

"No, I'll make it. I have two hours at lunchtime tomorrow. I can take a nap."

"I don't think you should." Byron looked worried.

"I'll be all right, really." Genie smiled. It was nice to have someone besides Portia fuss over her. Which reminded her. "What was that about Portia having a party?"

"Oh, yes. That's next Saturday. She said it was to be an Arabian Nights costume party. Do you want to go? I'm game if you are."

"I guess so," Genie replied. Portia, she knew, would keep after her unmercifully until she gave in, anyway, but the idea of going to one of Portia's elaborate parties with Byron made her tired nerves tingle in a combination of apprehension and excitement.

"Good. We'll talk about that later, then. I'd better be getting home. Are you sure you're all right?"

"I'm fine. Very strong and healthy."

Byron smiled, his eyes so warm that Genie could feel the current reach her from where he stood. She wanted desperately to jump up and fling her arms around him, but something told her that she had better not. When Byron spoke, she knew he was feeling the same way. "I'm not going to touch you again until I'm sure neither of us is going to react the wrong way," he said, "so stop looking at me like a forlorn kitten."

"I'm not," Genie denied, frowning.

"You are," Byron contradicted. "Get to sleep. Good night."

With that he turned and left the room. Moments later, Genie heard the front door close behind him. She got to her feet and looked out the window, forgetting that with the lights on he could see her. When he reached the road, he looked toward the house and waved. She waved back and watched him jog off up the hill. It made her feel lonely, watching him go, but it wasn't so bad this time, she thought. He'd be back. And maybe sometime, before very long if she was lucky, he wouldn't have to leave at all.

She turned from the window and began to undress. Could Portia be right? Was it kismet? Love at first sight? If it was, could they overcome their fears, marry and have a family? Would anything ever dim the sorrow Byron felt over losing his first little son, never even finding him?

"Oh, my," Genie murmured aloud. Tim. Tim had been born only a few months before that terrible earthquake. As far as anyone knew, he had been born in Mexico City, or near there. No one had been sure exactly when or where, so Portia and Mark had given him June first for a birthday. They were told that he had been found after the quake by rescuers, then taken to a hospital. When no family claimed him by Christmas, he had been put up for adoption. The Donaldsons were next on the agency's list. Portia, with her penchant for cosmic signs, had taken the child with enthusiasm. What more perfect sign was there than to be offered a child on Christmas day? But what if there had been some slipup, and the authorities had checked in the wrong places? Tim couldn't be Byron's missing son, could he? She remembered the intense way he had studied Tim, the morning he ran into her car. Was he thinking . . . ?

Genie shook her head impatiently and slipped beneath her bedcovers. Of course not. He was wondering if Tim was her son. Besides, Byron would have checked every possible place for his baby son. There must have been many children orphaned in that terrible disaster. Tim did look quite a bit like a child of Byron's might look by now, with a mother like Byron had described, but so would many little boys with Mexican or part-Mexican ancestry. It must be doubly hard for Byron to see children that reminded him so forcibly of what he had lost. He had recovered quickly, though, and smiled when Tim called him a pirate. He must be used to that kind of shock. There were so many children of Mexican ancestry in Southern California.

If we had children, they wouldn't have black hair, Genie thought, yawning and stretching luxuriously. It would be nice if they had those beautiful dark eyes, though. Not that it was likely to happen. Unless that shooting star had been right.

CHAPTER FOUR

A FEW DAYS LATER, Genie was not feeling nearly so hopeful. She was not even certain that Byron would return. It made her both miserable and irritated with herself for feeling that way.

"I feel as if I'm living on top of a cactus plant," she told Portia the following Wednesday, when asked why she was such a grump about going to a costume shop to pick out something glamorous for the party. "I itch and twitch all the time. I wish Byron would at least call. For all I know, he's decided not to go to your party, after all."

"I'm sure he'll come, but if you're so worried why don't you call him? Telephones do work both ways, you know," Portia said, giving her a sideways glance.

"I'm waiting for your cosmic forces, or can't they handle it alone?" Genie said sarcastically. "I noticed you didn't let them."

"You mean because I decided to have an Arabian Nights party and invite Byron to bring you?" Portia asked, smiling benignly. "Why dear, that was sheer cosmic inspiration. Tim happened to pick up a beautifully illustrated book of those stories at the library. One of the characters reminded me of Byron. Yes, cosmic forces. I'm simply their tool."

"Then I must be their fool," Genie said bitterly. She could not get Byron out of her mind for more than a few minutes at a time, but she needed to see him, to know that the way he made her feel was real. That was the only way she was going to overcome her fears, and she wanted to get on with it, which made her feel vaguely disloyal to Kurt's memory. "Maybe I should wear this jester suit," she said, holding up a bright-colored outfit with jingling bells on the jagged-edged sleeves.

"Don't be ridiculous. How about this? You'd make a wonderful belly dancer with that trim midriff of yours," Portia said, dangling a gold-fringed outfit in front of Genie. "I'll have some perfect music for it."

"No, thanks," Genie said, frowning. "Too bare."

"Don't be such a prude."

"No way! I am not going to make a spectacle of myself," Genie said snappishly.

"It's a good thing I came with you," Portia said, eyeing her sister critically. "You'd probably have picked out a shroud and a veil." She rummaged through the rack of costumes. "Here it is!" she said triumphantly, pulling out a gauzy costume with layers of floating veils in shades of pink and gold, edged in sequins. "You can be Scheherazade!"

Genie made a wry face. "That's not too bad," she said.

"Try it on," Portia commanded.

With a sigh, Genie took the costume into the dressing room and put it on. Beneath the layers of veils was a stretchy flesh-colored leotard, which they were attached to. It had only one shoulder strap, enabling the veils to appear to swirl around as she turned. It did look quite nice, she thought, and she had gold sandals at home that would go with it well.

"How does it look?" she asked, returning to show Portia the results.

"Perfect, if you didn't look so depressed," Portia replied, "but I expect when you have Byron at your side you'll look quite different."

Genie made a face at her and returned to put on her own slacks and T-shirt. "Now that that's decided, I'd better get back to the club," she said a few minutes later. "I've got two more lessons this afternoon."

"Call Byron tonight," Portia advised her. "It's bad for your health to go around all tied up in knots."

"I'll take some extra vitamins," Genie told her. "Heaven only knows when these knots will untie."

Genie finished her day at the club, then drove home in the old clunker that the garage had loaned her while they repaired her car. It coughed and gasped its way up the hill to her house, threatening to expire before it reached her driveway.

"Will I ever be glad to get rid of you," she told it with a grimace, slamming the door behind her. "You'd never make it to Byron's house." She looked up the hill and shook her head. For all she knew, Byron didn't even live there anymore. She went into the house, fed the cats and then fixed herself a microwave dinner. "I wonder what Byron would think if he knew I can't cook," she mused, poking at her dinner listlessly. He probably wouldn't care. She tossed out the cardboard container, then paced restlessly around the house, out on the deck, then back inside, Ms. Kitty following her with frequent meows as if she wondered what was wrong with her mistress.

Maybe Portia was right, Genie thought, pausing by the kitchen telephone and tapping her fingers on the counter. No. She didn't want to talk to Byron, she wanted to see him. The idea made her feel even more tense, but she'd be more tense soon, anyway, if he didn't come to see her. She could drive up to his house. No. That blasted car probably wouldn't make it. She could walk. Her feet felt like two hot bricks after the long day on the courts, but they would make it.

"I'll put on my old tennis shoes," she muttered. Sandals were hard on the feet, especially walking uphill. She went into her room, slipped into her comfortable old shoes, then started resolutely off, ignoring the butterflies in her stomach. She noticed that the houses, as she climbed farther up the hill, were more and more elegant, the result of the increasingly exclusive price of the area. Byron must have paid a pretty penny for his, she thought when she reached his driveway. He had a lot of land. His house was set back so far that it couldn't even be seen from the road.

She walked up the curving driveway, then stopped, stunned by the beauty of the house. It seemed to spring from the side of the mountain, its sweeping cantilevered decks and expanses of glass giving it an airy look, as if it had flown in and alighted on the spot rather than being built there. There was not much lawn, only a few feet surrounding the circular area where Byron's car was parked, most of the area having been kept wild and natural looking, although it did look as if it were tended to keep it from getting out of hand. It was, Genie thought, a perfect house for Byron de Stefano.

There was a door at ground level, but it looked little used. A stairway led from a path to the right of the door to one of the wide decks. Genie guessed that was the way Byron usually used to enter his house. Well, he never knocked on her door. She might as well go up to the deck and surprise him, too.

Her tennis shoes made no sound on the wide redwood staircase. When she reached the top, she paused and looked around. The view over the treetops was lovely. The glass wall next to the deck where she stood was covered by soft-

looking, loosely woven beige draperies. A little farther on,
she could see a screen door. She walked slowly down the
deck to the doorway. Here the curtains were pulled back,
and the door behind the screen was open. She could see into
a large, high-ceilinged room with a free-standing circular
fireplace in the center. It was obviously the living room,
rather more formal than Genie would have expected, full of
soft upholstered chairs and sofas in neutral colors, and tables and cabinets of teak. There was no one in sight. Genie
had just lifted her hand to try the door when she heard
voices, and she pulled back behind the part of the glass
covered by the draperies, feeling trapped and uncomfortable. She didn't want to barge in on Byron if he had company. Maybe she should try to sneak back down the stairs.
If they came out on the deck . . .

The voices drew nearer. One was unmistakably Byron's
deep voice, the other the voice of a woman. They were
chattering rapidly to each other in Spanish, which Genie
could not understand, although their tone suggested that
they were arguing, probably about money. The word *dollars* came through loud and clear several times. Maybe it
was Byron's maid. He surely must have one to take care of
this place. And then again—a sick knot formed in Genie's
stomach—it might be something less innocent. Terrified of
being discovered eavesdropping, even though she couldn't
understand, Genie turned and crept back along the deck
and down the stairs as fast as she could. She had just
reached the bottom when she heard the sliding screen door
to the deck open and then slide shut with a thud, followed
by footsteps on the deck, heading toward the stairs.

"Oh, God," Genie muttered, her heart pounding. If she
had only worn green instead of red she could try to blend
in with the shrubbery below the deck, but as it was . . . A
sudden inspiration hit her and she sprinted quickly the few

steps to the ground-level door, raised her hand and knocked just as she heard footsteps on the stairs behind her. She knocked again, and turned when the footsteps reached the bottom of the stairs.

"Oh, there you... are," she said, the smile she had prepared dying on her face. Standing beside Byron was one of the most beautiful women she had ever seen, dressed in an elegant black suit, her black hair swept back in a severe style that accented the perfect oval of her face and set off the huge diamond pendants dangling from her ears. She was holding a black carry-on bag. Byron was handsomer than ever, wearing a white shirt and dark blue pants, a matching suitcoat thrown over one arm and a suitcase in his hand.

At the sight of Genie, Byron stopped, stock-still, his face pale beneath his tan. "Genie. This is a surprise," he said after staring at her in apparent confusion for several moments.

"Yes, I, uh, guess it is," Genie replied. She felt unbelievably small, insignificant and stupid standing before the two elegant-looking people. "I...thought I'd come and say hello," she said lamely, when Byron seemed to have nothing to contribute. "I see that you're leaving."

Byron roused himself. "Yes. I tried to call you a few minutes ago. I'm afraid I won't be able to make the party on Saturday, after all. I've got to make an unexpected trip to Mexico. Something important—that is, some personal business I have to take care of. I—I did get hold of Portia. She was to tell you."

"I see," Genie said. Personal business. Yes, it probably was very personal. But business? That was a laugh. She also doubted that he'd tried to call her. He'd probably left that chore to her sister. She watched, anger beginning to simmer, as Byron turned toward his companion and said something to her in Spanish, probably, she thought, an explanation of who this tacky-looking person in the red warm-up suit was. The woman listened, then looked at Genie and smiled, a cool, sophisticated smile that displayed incredibly perfect white teeth.

"Genie," Byron said, "this is Elisa de Cordova, my late wife's sister."

Oh, is it really? Genie thought skeptically. *I'm sure that's why you looked so guilty when you saw me.* Nevertheless, she managed to smile politely. "Tell her that I'm happy to meet her."

Byron spoke to the woman in Spanish again, and she said something to Genie that Genie assumed was the same sort of greeting in Spanish.

Genie smiled again and inclined her head as graciously as she could. "I guess I'll be getting on home," she said to Byron. "Have a nice trip." *And don't bother to come and see me when you get back,* her thoughts continued.

"Where's your car?" Byron asked, frowning.

"I walked," Genie replied. "My car's being fixed and I didn't trust the one they loaned me to make it up the hill this far."

"It's too bad my car will only take two people," Byron said, still frowning.

"Don't let it bother you. I'm quite capable of walking. It's downhill all the way," Genie said coolly. She'd had quite enough of this polite chitchat. She nodded to the two tall dark-haired people. "Goodbye," she said, then turned and walked briskly away, her jaw set and her clenched hands swinging along at her sides. She had only gone a short way down the hill when Byron's car pulled up beside her. She stopped and raised her eyebrows at Byron questioningly.

"Genie," he said, his forehead creased in a worried frown, "be sure and go to that party of Portia's and have a good time. I'm really sorry that I can't be with you."

"Don't give it another thought," Genie said stonily. *And get out of here before I scream!*

Byron's mouth pursed in a down-turned line. "Don't look at me like that, Genie," he said softly.

Fighting for control, Genie jerked her chin up defiantly. "Just go away," she said tightly, then started running on down the hill. Moments later, Byron's car shot past her. She waited until it was out of sight, then stopped running. Silent tears poured down her cheeks as she trudged on home. It was over now, all over. She never wanted to see Byron de Stefano again!

Back at her house, Genie flung open the screen door to her own small deck and threw herself down on the comfortable old lounge chair and sobbed into its faded green cushion. What did she expect? She should have known that Byron wasn't the type to spend his life alone. He might be afraid of a permanent companion, but with his wealth and fame he could have anyone he wanted for something temporary. His sister-in-law? Hah! If she was, why hadn't he brought her to meet her? Was he ashamed of poor Genie Compton, a second-rate tennis player with a plain middle-class family? Or was he sorry that he'd ever told her about his sad memories, regretting that he'd heard about hers, too? Why would he want to bother with someone who was just as messed up as he was? Someone like Elisa de Cordova would be a lot more fun. She looked as if she could pay her own way, and Byron's, too, if she wanted.

Something furry climbed over Genie's shoulder and poked an experimental paw into her ear. Genie reached up and took hold of the kitten.

"Oh, it's you," she said to the calico kitten. "He can't have you, either," she said, holding it close to her nose. "He'd go off on some jaunt and forget you were even there. You deserve a better home than that."

There was the sound of a car stopping in the driveway, and then a door opening and shutting.

"Oh, Lord," Genie muttered, grabbing the bottom of her sweatshirt and mopping her eyes. It could be the garage returning her car. They had said it might be finished this afternoon and if it was they'd bring it back. She got to her feet just as Portia came through the carport door in a swirl of bright colors, Tim chugging along behind her.

"There you are," Portia said breathlessly. "I tried to call you a little while ago, and I even tried Sondra's to see if you were there."

"I went for a walk," Genie said, smiling at Tim, who had quickly found his favorite yellow kitten and picked it up. She knew why Portia had come. Thank goodness she'd already found out and gotten over the worst of the shock. It wouldn't do to break down in front of Tim, who lived with the illusion that Aunt Genie could do most anything. Now, if she could keep Portia from noticing her puffy eyes... She kept her face averted, watching Tim hugging the kitten.

"Let's go in and have a glass of iced tea or something," Portia said, her voice high-pitched and anxious. "I've got something to tell you."

"I already know, but come on in and have a drink, anyway," Genie replied, whirling around and going toward the door ahead of Portia. "Do you want a Coke, Tim?"

"Sure," Tim replied.

"You know?" Portia sounded surprised. "You're certainly taking it well. I thought..." She bustled into the kitchen and managed to get in front of Genie. "Oh, no, you're not," she said. "How did you find out?"

"I went to Byron's house," Genie replied, pulling out the ice-cube bin. "He told me."

"Well, he said it couldn't be helped," Portia said. "I expect a man as important and famous as he is does have business all over the world."

"I expect so," Genie agreed. "I expect he has women all over the world, too. He had one with him. Beautiful. Mexican. They were talking Spanish, so I couldn't understand what they said, but it was obvious they knew each other well." She plunked three ice cubes viciously into each of their glasses. "He had the nerve to say she was his late wife's sister."

"His late wife was Mexican?"

"Yes."

"Well, then, isn't it possible?"

"Possible, but not likely. He looked as guilty as sin when he discovered me at his door," Genie said, handing a can of Coke to Tim.

Portia frowned as Genie jerked the tea carafe from the refrigerator and spilled a large puddle of tea on the counter as she tried to pour it. "Here, let me do that," she said. "Go and sit down. You're a wreck."

"No, I'm not," Genie denied snappishly. "I'm doing fine. I'm very glad I found out about Byron de Stefano before any more time passed. I want nothing more to do with him. And don't give me any more of your nonsense about cosmic forces. That's a lot of you-know-what."

"Oh, certainly," Portia said sarcastically, grabbing a sponge to wipe the counter as Genie picked up the dripping glasses. "That's why you're so upset. I sometimes wonder how anyone's mind can work in such convoluted paths as yours does. Maybe you should make an appointment to talk to Grover Aldrich professionally."

"Portia," Genie said warningly, "I am perfectly fine. I may have been confused for a while, but I'm not anymore."

"Good," Portia said, following her to the table. "Then you'll be happy to come to the party without Byron, won't you? You'll have fun without him. There'll be some single men there, and you'll enjoy their company, just like any normal, unconfused woman would."

Genie glared at her sister. "That was a low blow," she said. "You know I hate going to parties alone."

"Alone or with anyone but Byron," Portia retorted. "But you *will* come. I've invited Sondra and Sam, and I'll send them to get you. Sam's big enough to see that you come, even if he has to carry you."

"I don't want to come," Genie repeated sulkily, knowing she was fighting a losing battle. Why was it Portia always came out on top in situations like this? Ever since they were children, Portia had manipulated her into doing things she didn't want to do, even convincing her that she was happy to take the blame for some scrape that was Portia's fault. She had even entered her first tennis tournament because Portia sent in her name and the entry fee. She had often thought that she won, in spite of her shaking knees, because Portia said she had to so as not to embarrass their father. Was she a wimp, or was Portia always right?

"You've gotta come and see my costume," Tim put in, coming to stand beside her chair. "I'm going to be a slave driver."

"I can't miss that," Genie said, smiling and brushing back the dark hair that perennially flopped onto his forehead. "All right, I'll come." She made a face at Portia. "You don't need to send Mark after me."

"Good," Portia said, getting up from the table. "I've got to run. They didn't have anything to fit Mark at the costume shop and I'm trying to turn him into a sultan."

"Can I take Monster home yet?" Tim asked hopefully.

"After the party," Genie promised. "I expect your mother's got a lot to do until then."

"Can we get him Sunday?" Tim looked at his mother, his dark eyes wide. "Can we?"

"If I have time to get him a litter box by then," Portia said. "Come along. We've got lots to do."

After Portia and Tim had left, Genie drifted back out onto the deck and leaned on the railing, staring into the gathering dusk. Alone again. She hated the terrible ache inside her. If only Byron—

"Stop that!" she scolded herself, angrily dashing a tear from her cheek. She couldn't mope over Byron forever. Or Kurt, either. She should try to be more like her sister, always making plans, pushing ahead. Portia had such a wonderful life, especially since Tim had come into it. She had married Mark, ten years older than she, right after college. Now Portia was thirty, only three years older than Genie. If Genie didn't get her act together pretty soon, life was going to pass her by. She used to have fun, loved to go out and party. With or without Byron de Stefano, she was going to have to start having fun again. And Portia's party was the place to do it. Maybe she'd go back and get that belly-dancer's costume, after all. If only she knew how to belly dance, she might surprise everyone!

CHAPTER FIVE

"YOU DON'T HAPPEN to have a tape on belly dancing, do you?" Genie asked the clerk in the video store the next afternoon.

She had already exchanged her Scheherazade costume for the scanty outfit with its tiny gold-fringed, flesh-colored bra and the gold sequined bikini attached to diaphanous turquoise harem pants. There was an ankle-length sleeveless robe of the same turquoise material that went with it, but did little to disguise the scantiness of the rest of the costume. Turning back and forth in front of the dressing-room mirror, Genie had smiled to herself in satisfaction. She was going to turn over a new leaf with a vengeance. Wouldn't Portia be surprised!

"Oh, yes," the clerk said, going to a rack containing assorted fitness tapes. "A lot of women use this to trim their midsections these days. It's great exercise." His eyes scanned Genie's trim form. "Not that you need it," he said.

Genie smiled. "Thanks. I just want to be able to fake a reasonable dance."

"This will do it," the clerk promised.

That night, she put the tape on the VCR and watched the dark-haired teacher and two assistants demonstrating the various moves. It didn't look too hard. She began to follow along, swaying and undulating in time to the music. It was fun. A couple of days' practice and she'd be ready.

On Saturday evening, Genie put her hair up in a tower-
ing topknot wrapped with turquoise satin ribbon, with
tendrils of ribbon streaming down the back. She used eye-
liner and shadow to make her eyes look slanted and mysterious. She tried the dance routine in costume before she
left for the party. The dozen inexpensive gold and silver
bangles she had bought to wear on her arms sparkled and
tinkled. Yes, she was definitely ready. The new Genie
Compton was going to knock them dead. Too bad about
Byron de Stefano. She hoped he was having fun in Mexico
with Elisa, but she doubted it was all that thrilling. Elisa
had looked like rather a cold fish.

Genie's heart was tripping with excitement when she
parked her car near Mark and Portia's house at nine
o'clock that evening. Cars were already lining the street, for
the party had started at eight. Genie had waited, wanting
to make a proper entrance. She got out and walked toward
the house. Light was streaming from the windows of the
strikingly modern structure, which always reminded Genie
of a pile of glittering white ice cubes, stacked by a remark-
ably clever giant. As she drew near, she could hear the
sound of exotic music over the rumble of voices, and she
smiled to herself. It was the same music as on the tape she
had rented. Rather than slip in unannounced as she might
have done only recently, she rang the doorbell. When Mark
opened the door she gave him what she hoped was a mysterious and seductive smile.

"Hello, Mark," she purred, slipping off her long outer
garment and handing it to him. "Sorry I'm late."

Mark stared at her open-mouthed. "Wow!" he said finally. "That's a . . . a great costume, Genie."

"Thank you. I like yours, too." Mark wore a white satin
turban trimmed with fake jewels, and a voluminous robe of
gold satin over a white satin shirt and pants.

"Come on in and dazzle the guests," Mark said. "I'll get you a drink and introduce you to everyone you don't know. And I'd better find Portia. She'll want to check out that costume, too."

Mark barreled off toward the back of the house, his robe billowing behind him. Genie moved slowly into the living room, enjoying the stares of the familiar guests, especially Grover Aldrich, who looked first as if he had seen a ghost and then broke into a positively lecherous grin. He arrived at her side just as Mark returned.

"You look absolutely…radiant tonight, Genie," he said, his eyes traipsing up and down her form as if he had never seen her before.

"Why, thank you, Grover," Genie said sweetly. "Wait until you see my dance." She took the drink that Mark handed her. "What is this?" she inquired, taking a sip. "It's delicious."

"Portia calls it Scheherazade Punch," Mark replied. "Watch out. It's not as innocent as it looks."

"Lots of things aren't," Genie said, giving him a coy smile. "Did you find Portia?"

Mark glanced around. "Here she comes."

Portia, resplendent in a feminine version of Mark's costume, took one look at Genie and stopped dead, her mouth dropping open in amazement. "Is that you?" she croaked.

Genie burst out laughing. Seeing her sister's response made the effort worth it. "Of course it's me," she said. "I've decided to become my own cosmic force. I'll be ready to do my dance. At least, in a little while. I have to meet some people first." She smiled up at Mark and took hold of his arm. "Are you ready to introduce me around?"

"You bet," he said. "I'll tell them you're part of my harem."

For over an hour, Genie moved among the guests, sipping her punch, pleased that everyone responded to her as if she really was someone quite new and different. Sam ogled her so obviously that Sondra gave his arm a vicious pinch. Even Tim, whose tanned little body looked adorable in baggy harem pants, a plastic scimitar dangling from a wide belt and a tiny red satin bolero, seemed to think his aunt had a new image.

"Are you really going to dance, Aunt Genie?" he asked, coming up to her as she was talking to a handsome, golden-haired young architect. "Dad says you are. Can I dance with you?"

"A real belly dance?" the architect asked, his blue eyes taking on a new gleam as Genie nodded. "This I've got to see. What music do you want? I'll tell Portia to put it on."

Genie was not quite sure afterward how it all happened. The architect disappeared. Then people began to murmur and look toward her. A space was cleared in the middle of the living room floor. Mark came in and took her ceremoniously by the hand, led her to the space and bowed.

"Ladies and gentlemen," he announced, "we are fortunate to have with us this evening a *real* genie, a princess of the realm, whose magical skills at the dance have entranced kings and princes from all over the world." He let go of Genie's hand, backed away, then clapped his hands. "Let the music begin."

The music started. Genie began the routine, finding it even more pleasant than she had at home, her hips seeming almost disconnected from the rest of her. She smiled flirtatiously at the men as she turned and swayed seductively. When the music stopped, she put her hands together and bowed deeply to enthusiastic applause. "Encore," someone called, and the rest of the group joined in.

"Well, just one more," she said graciously.

The music had just begun when she noticed a small commotion near the front door. She kept dancing, watching out of the corner of her eye as the crowd parted to let someone through. A very late comer, she thought, turning toward the handsome architect and giving her hips an extra wiggle. He grinned and blew her a kiss. She smiled and made a come-hither gesture with her hands, then turned coyly away. Her eyes fell next on Portia. She was not smiling. She looked apprehensive. She had her head turned toward her left, but her eyes were darting back and forth between Genie and someone else.

Even before she turned her head just enough so that she could see who Portia was looking at, Genie felt her pulse quicken. When she saw, her heart lurched and she suddenly felt as if she could not breathe. Byron was standing at the edge of her little dance floor, staring at her. He was wearing ordinary street clothes, but his expression was anything but ordinary. He looked both absolutely furious and completely stunned.

A surge of anxiety washed through Genie and left her trembling. Her heart pounded so loudly that she could scarcely hear the music. She could not tear her eyes from Byron's face, but she kept on dancing, her chin lifted defiantly, while inside her a fierce battle went on between a feeling of guilt and one of resentment. Byron de Stefano had no right to stare at her like that. She had only done what he told her. She was having a good time! Too bad if he didn't like it, after what he'd done.

It seemed forever before the music stopped and Genie again took a bow. The crowd closed in immediately. The architect arrived at her side and put his arms around her just as Byron appeared in front of her, the furious part of his expression having taken over from the stunned. Genie glanced hurriedly up at the golden-haired architect.

"This is Byron de Stefano," she said to him, trying desperately to remember the man's name. "Byron, this is, uh..."

"Clint Steger," the architect provided with an easy grin. He held out his hand to Byron. "I like your work."

"Thanks," Byron said, giving the man's hand a brief shake while his eyes remained on Genie, so fiery in their intensity that she felt as if they were boring right through her.

"Clint's an architect," Genie offered, wishing that she could suddenly disappear like a real genie. "He did the new wing at the club."

"Nice job," Byron said politely, scarcely glancing in the man's direction. "I came straight from the airport," he said to Genie, his tone accusing.

"So I gathered," Genie replied, frowning. He had no business glaring at her like that. She looked up at Clint. "People hate to miss Portia's parties."

"I don't blame them," Clint said, an amused smile playing about his lips. "Too bad you didn't get here earlier and see Genie's first dance," he said to Byron.

"It certainly is," Byron replied.

Byron, Genie observed, gave Clint a look that would have killed an elephant. Was he actually jealous? If so, it was rather fun getting even. She smiled at him sweetly. "Have a nice trip?"

"Very tiring, but I got a lot accomplished," Byron said.

Mark appeared and thrust a glass of punch into Byron's hand. "Have some of Portia's latest concoction," he said.

Byron glanced at the glass, then tossed it down in one gulp and handed the glass back to Mark. "I need to talk to you," he said to Genie, shooting a meaningful look in Clint's direction.

"We are talking, aren't we?" Genie said, maintaining her saccharine smile and fluttering her eyelashes at Byron innocently. It was, she realized immediately, the wrong thing to do. He let out a sort of growling sound and grabbed her upper arm in a viselike grip.

"Alone. Now," he said, pulling her away from Clint and toward the back of the house as fast as he could move through the crowd.

"Let go of me," Genie said in an undertone, at the same time trying not to look so angry that they'd attracted attention.

"Not on your life," Byron murmured back. He stopped by the doors that led to Mark and Portia's illuminated pool and looked at the crowd milling around outside. "Too many people," he said, heading toward the kitchen, where another group was gathered around Portia. Byron bent and whispered something in her ear. Portia's eyes lighted and she whispered something back, ignoring Genie's threatening glare. Byron nodded and resumed his march, through the laundry room and up a short flight of stairs that led to a small, deserted sitting room on a mezzanine level overlooking the pool. "This," he said, pulling Genie down beside him on a lavender love seat, "is more like it. Does Portia always have this many people at her parties?"

"Usually," Genie replied, rubbing her arm as Byron finally released it. "Mark's in the advertising business and knows a lot of people."

"Half of Los Angeles," Byron said dryly. He looked at Genie, his expression softening until at last he smiled. "Well, here we are," he said. "I wish I'd known I could make it back tonight."

The soft warmth of his eyes made Genie feel fluttery inside. She hadn't wanted to see him again, but now that he was here she was falling under his spell just as if he hadn't done anything wrong. She looked away and asked pointedly, "Things get dull south of the border?"

"No, but I was worried about you. You looked so upset when I told you I couldn't come tonight that I couldn't enjoy the few minutes when I wasn't tied up in meetings."

Was that why he thought she was upset? "Did you think I'd stay home and mope just because you had a better offer?" she asked coolly, giving him a sideways glance.

"A better offer?" Byron reached over and took hold of Genie's chin and turned her face toward his. "Are you talking about Elisa?" he asked, his eyebrows raised as if, Genie thought, he were amazed at the idea.

"Who else?" she said, trying unsuccessfully to jerk her chin free.

"Genie, Elisa is my sister-in-law," Byron said, slowly and deliberately. "She's also a lawyer. She's been handling some rather delicate business matters for me lately."

"Hah!" Genie retorted. "That doesn't explain anything." She tried to push Byron's hand away, but he caught her hand and held it tightly.

"What would you like me to explain?" he asked softly, pulling her toward him.

The bright lights glittering in the depths of Byron's dark eyes were threatening to blind Genie, luring her toward them with a dangerous siren song that drowned out her hard-won common sense. That song, she reminded herself, was no celestial refrain. It was simply a very handsome man using his powers of seduction. Powers he obviously was very practiced at using. She pulled back against his hand and shook her head. "I shouldn't have to tell you," she said. "You didn't call or come to see me for days. Then you had to leave so suddenly that you couldn't let me know until you were practically on the plane. I don't believe a word of your story."

She trembled as Byron, smiling, traced a finger along her cheek and under her chin. "Don't do that," she said crossly, tossing her head back and looking down her nose at him. "You don't seem to get the picture. I'm angry with you, and I haven't heard one word of explanation yet. I expect that's because you can't think of any."

Byron grinned. "No, it's because you look so beautiful tonight I'm having a devil of a time thinking at all." At Genie's unladylike muttered expletive he laughed. "All right. You're not going to like the explanation, but you may as well get used to it because it's not the last time you'll hear it.

"When I went home from your house—I guess it was a week ago today, wasn't it?—I wasn't in the mood to sleep, so I started in on a painting. As sometimes happens when things go well, I got so completely involved that I didn't realize the passage of time. I don't sleep or eat normally, either. I take short naps on a cot in my studio. My house-keeper brings me food now and then. I thought of calling you several times, but it was always either when you were at work or in the middle of the night. On Wednesday morning, Elisa showed up with some information I'd asked for. I didn't take her interruption very well, and I was furious when she insisted I'd have to go with her to deal with some officials. I'd reached the point where I was planning to come and get you later that day to see what I'd been working on, but no, she already had the plane tickets and some appointments set up." Byron stopped and sighed, shaking his head at Genie's still-sulky expression. "I knew you wouldn't like it," he said, caressing her cheek again with his fingertips, "but believe me, it's true."

Genie studied him thoughtfully. She might not like the explanation, she thought, but she could believe it. Kurt had gotten involved like that sometimes in his laboratory, not even knowing what day it was, forgetting to call. She had finally convinced him that she would rather hear from him at three in the morning than not at all. If she was going to go on with Byron, she would have to make him understand that, too, if he could. But... did she want to go on? Or would she rather try to forget both him and Kurt, intense, driven men. Exciting men. And find someone more ordinary, less upsetting.

She closed her eyes and tried to imagine that dramatic, handsome face before her disappearing from her life forever, fading into the mists below her deck on some chill, foggy morning. Like a deep warning bell, she felt the ache of loneliness tug at her heart. She was trapped. She couldn't bear the thought. She opened her eyes and blinked back a blur of tears.

"I believe you," she said hoarsely, "only next time, call me even if it's the middle of the night. Call me at work. I was afraid..." She choked back a sob. "I was afraid you didn't want to see me again."

"Oh, Genie," Byron said softly, pulling her into his arms and holding her close. "Don't ever think that. I'll call. And if I don't, I hereby give you permission I've given to no one else to call me. Even if I'm in the middle of the greatest thing since the *Mona Lisa,* I promise I won't yell at you, and if you come to see me, I won't throw anything at you."

Genie could hear the smile in his voice and pulled her head back to see it. "I guess I sound kind of silly and insecure," she said, the warmth she saw in his eyes wrapping comforting tendrils around her heart.

Byron shook his head. "I'd feel the same way," he said. His eyes drifted down to her mouth. He brushed her lips

softly with his and then looked back into her eyes again.
"May I take you home?" he asked. "We can come back for
your car tomorrow."

The dizzying implication of what Byron was asking made
Genie's already racing heart skip. He wanted to spend the
night with her. He had said he wouldn't touch her again
until he was sure they were both ready, no longer afraid.
Was he sure now? Was she? Not really, but she was sure
that she wanted him close, wanted to feel his arms around
her for more than a brief moment. And she had decided it
was time to be bolder, not shrink from life anymore. She
had begun today. She might as well keep on and see where
it led.

"I'd like that," she said, smiling and touching his cheek
with her hand.

"Good." Byron smiled radiantly, his arms tightening
around her. His mouth descended on hers again, this time
with no soft preamble, demanding and passionate. Genie
felt the flash fires within her ignite in response, her lips
parting instantly to welcome the assault. Suddenly every
inch of her felt more alive. The touch of Byron's hands on
her bare back seemed to penetrate the very core of her being, caressing a part of her that no one else had ever
touched. She murmured soft sounds of pleasure and held
him close, loving the feel of his strength surrounding her.

"Hi!" said a high little voice.

As if they had been doused with a bucket of cold water,
Genie and Byron pulled apart.

"Hi, yourself," Byron said, recovering first and grinning at Tim, who was standing beside them in his striped
pajamas. "Looks like you're ready for bed."

"Yeah. I've got to find my mom to tuck me in," Tim
said. He looked at Genie. "Have you seen her lately?"

"She was in the kitchen a little while ago," Genie replied.

"Tell you what," Byron said. "We're leaving now, and we have to find your mom, too, to say goodbye. We can find her together."

"Okay," Tim said, suddenly climbing onto Byron's lap and putting his arms around his neck. "Carry me," he ordered. "I don't want any of those big people to step on my bare feet."

"Good idea," Byron agreed, with a grin at Genie. He stood up and tucked Tim easily against his hip.

Tim reached up and tugged experimentally at Byron's hair. "How come your hair's so long?" he asked.

"Because I like it that way," Byron replied.

As he looked down at the little boy and smiled, Genie felt a painful tug at her heart. They did look as if they could be father and son. Byron was so good with him. How terribly sad that he had lost his own child.

"I wish I could have long hair," Tim said as they started down the stairs.

Byron wrinkled his nose at Tim. "No, you don't. It's a nuisance when you're little. Gets dirty all the time, and then you have to have your mother wash it and dry it. Wait until you're older."

"How much older?"

"You'd better check that out with your mother," Byron replied. "I don't want to get in trouble with her."

They found Portia back in the living room near the piano, where one of the guests was playing some of the music from *Kismet*.

"I believe there's a demand for tucking in," Byron said, delivering Tim to her. "Genie and I are about to leave, too."

Portia raised her eyebrows questioningly at Genie, who leaned over and whispered in her ear, "We'll come back for my car tomorrow."

At that Portia's eyebrows hopped a notch higher and then she smiled knowingly. "Have a nice evening," she said. "Tim, stop that! What is it?" The little boy was tugging at her sleeve insistently.

"I want to know when I can let my hair get long," he said.

Byron smiled ruefully. "I'm afraid I've started something."

Portia shrugged resignedly. "I thought I wouldn't have to cope with that until he's a teenager, but he's been after me ever since he met the pirate with the fancy car."

"I told him to wait until he can keep it clean himself," Byron said, "so you have a little reprieve."

"Mr. de Stefano's right," Portia said to Tim. "It's hard work, taking care of long hair so that it looks as nice as his. When you get so that you can keep your room nice and clean, I'll think about it." Her eyes twinkled merrily. "That ought to give me a lot of time," she said.

"Just about forever, if he's like you used to be," Genie teased. "Well, good night. It's been a lovely party."

"Good night," Portia said, giving Genie's arm a squeeze. "Stop in when you come back for your car. We'll just be lying around, recovering."

"You're going to catch cold in that costume," Byron remarked a few minutes later as they walked down the street to his car. "That cloak is about as substantial as a cobweb."

"I'm not cold," Genie said. In fact, she felt as if her skin were on fire from the touch of Byron's arm around her.

"You will be when we get going," he said, giving her a hug. "I can't keep my arm around you in those bucket seats."

When they reached his Ferrari, he took off his suit coat. "Put this on," he said, holding it up for her. "It'll not only keep you warm, it will probably prevent an accident." At Genie's questioning look he grinned. "If anyone saw you in that outfit, they'd never look at the road again."

Genie made a face at him as she slipped into the jacket. "I've always wanted to stop traffic," she said.

"That costume would do it," Byron smiled. As he slid into the driver's seat he looked over at Genie. "I'm going to have to trade this car in for something more romantic," he said. "Having a Ferrari isn't all it's cracked up to be."

"What do you mean?" Genie asked, puzzled. "It looks pretty special to me. I've never even ridden in one before."

"I mean the bucket seats," Byron replied as he got the car under way with a powerful surge of acceleration. "My dad's old pickup truck with the bench seat was a lot better for snuggling a date."

Genie laughed. "I'll bet you made good use of it, too," she said. "How did your father happen to have a pickup truck? I thought you were a city boy."

"I am. My dad owns a small grocery store in Brooklyn. We used the truck to get fresh produce and make deliveries. I got to use it on Saturday night if I cleaned it up." He grinned at Genie. "Sometimes it was worth it and sometimes it wasn't."

"I'll bet you had a lot of good times in it," Genie said. She could picture a young Byron de Stefano, picking up his latest high-school sweetheart in the shining clean truck. It might not have been a limousine, but with his charm, almost any girl would have thought it was.

"That I did," Byron replied. "For a few years. Then, when I started art school, my next younger brother took it over. And then the next."

"How many of you are there?" Genie asked. Byron seemed so much a law unto himself that she had thought he might be an only child.

"Six," Byron answered. "Four boys and two girls. My youngest sister's younger than you are. She's only twenty-one."

"A nice big family," Genie commented. "Portia and I are the only two in ours. Tell me, did your father expect you to go into the business with him, or was he happy about you choosing to be an artist?"

"My parents were all for it," Byron replied. "They love the arts, and the business wouldn't support all of us boys without expanding, which they've never wanted to do. They're happy with their neighborhood and their old friends. They'd have preferred I become some kind of musician, but I have a tin ear."

"Then they must have been pleased when you married a pianist," Genie said, immediately wishing she hadn't reminded him of that. The words had slipped out, following her train of thought. To her relief, Byron shrugged as if it didn't bother him.

"They loved Consuela's playing," he said, "but they weren't too crazy about her family. As you may have gathered from meeting Elisa, the de Cordovas consider themselves a cut above most people."

"She did seem rather...unbearably elegant," Genie said, searching for something appropriate to describe her impression.

Byron laughed. "A perfect description. How about your family? You said your father's a professor. What's his field?"

"English literature," Genie answered. "Medieval English literature, to be precise."

"You mean Chaucer and his ilk?" Byron asked.

"Exactly. My father's something of an expert on Chaucer. He's written a couple of books on him and he's in England researching another. He's not a stuffy sort of person, though. He can be a lot of fun. A good tennis player, too. A very stern taskmaster, though."

"Did he teach you to play?"

Genie nodded. "He was my first teacher. He got me started by offering me a hundred dollars if I could learn to play well enough to beat him."

"How long did that take?" Byron asked.

"I don't think I'll ever get quite that good," Genie replied, giving Byron a rueful little smile. "He can always distract me so that I start making stupid mistakes. It's more like psychological warfare, playing him."

Byron chuckled. "Fathers have a way of doing that, I think. I never was able to beat my father three straight games of chess, either."

They continued exchanging stories of their earlier years until they reached Genie's house.

"Maybe we should go on to my house," Byron suggested as he stopped his car in her driveway. "The neighbors might, uh, talk if they saw my car parked here all night."

Being reminded of what was about to happen made a small shiver run through Genie. Was she really ready for this? Her heart began to race. No, she wasn't, she thought, but she had been brooding earlier about the fact that she never seemed to be really ready for anything. She was not going to back out now.

"I hadn't thought of that," she said, frowning. "I suppose you're right. But I'll have to go in for a minute and put out the cats. I can put on some regular clothes, too. I don't think I'd want to come home in the morning in this outfit."

"That's a good thought," Byron agreed. "Let's do that, then. I haven't shown you the painting I've been working on, either. I—I'd like you to see it."

He seemed almost shy about it, Genie thought, smiling at him. "I'd like to see it," she said. "I've never seen a work in progress by a great artist."

Byron made a wry grimace. "Don't believe my publicity," he said. "I don't. Every time I start something new, I feel like a rank beginner."

"Then I'll pretend I'm looking at something by a rank but gifted beginner," Genie said. She got out of the car. "Do you want to come in or wait here?"

"I'll come with you," Byron said, getting out quickly and joining her. "I might lose my nerve and leave without you."

Genie looked up at him, surprised. "You, too?"

Byron nodded, then laughed. "We're a couple of terrible frauds, aren't we? Pretending to be such swingers. I've never been that way, in spite of what you might have thought, and I could tell by looking at you that you weren't, either."

"I'm not sure I'm glad that it's so obvious," Genie said with a sigh. "I've sometimes felt like I was born in the wrong century."

"So have I," Byron agreed. When Genie had opened the door and stepped inside, he took hold of her arm and turned her toward him. "Look," he said softly, "if you'd rather not . . ."

If she'd rather not? Genie stood motionless, scarcely breathing, drinking in the warmth of Byron's dark eyes like a tonic, the gentle concern that she read there filling her heart with a stronger desire than ever not to let this exceptional man vanish from her life, if she could help. "I—I'm not sure what I want," she said shakily. "I don't want to be alone."

"I don't, either," Byron said, touching her cheek with his fingertips. He released her arm. "Go and change your clothes, then. I'll round up the cats."

"All right," Genie said breathlessly. She hurried to her room. Her fingers trembled as she took off her flimsy costume and undid her elaborate topknot. She washed off her exotic makeup, brushed out her hair and then put on a simple blue chambray skirt with a matching top, decorated with a large red appliquéd flower. As an afterthought, she tucked her satin robe and some cosmetics into a straw tote bag, then returned to the living room, where Byron stood looking at some family pictures on the mantelpiece above the fireplace.

"You were a skinny little kid, weren't you?" he said, turning to her with a grin.

"The boys used to call me 'toothpick,'" Genie said with a grimace. "The ones that didn't call me 'bones.'"

"I'd call you 'beautiful,'" Byron said, coming to put his arm around her. "You look even more beautiful now than you did in that costume. Shall we go?"

Genie nodded, afraid to say anything for fear her voice would reveal her anxious state. She smiled up at Byron and let him lead her out into the night.

CHAPTER SIX

"THIS IS A BEAUTIFUL HOUSE." Genie felt that she had to say something ordinary to keep her mind from dwelling on the unusual situation she found herself in. Byron had said little on the short drive to his house. Perhaps, she thought, he was feeling a little strange, too. She was standing just inside the door from the deck in the large living room she had peeked into a few days before. The room looked even larger from inside, and she could now see that an open staircase led to an upper-level balcony. "This room is as big as some houses," she added, looking up at Byron.

"Yes, there's a lot of space," Byron said, glancing around the room with a curiously detached air. "Growing up in an apartment with eight people sharing one bathroom makes a person appreciate something like this. Would you like the grand tour?"

"Oh, yes," Genie said quickly. She wasn't sure she did want to see the house just then, but it was another way to give herself time to get her emotions under control, if they ever would be. She felt a little dizzy, as if she might suddenly discover none of this was real, the walls mere figments of her imagination that vanished when she tried to touch them. The man beside her was real enough, though. She could tell that from the shock wave that went through her when he took hold of her hand.

"Downstairs first, then," Byron said, leading her past the spectacular free-standing circular stone fireplace with a huge copper hood suspended above it. "There's an inside stairway behind that paneled wall." At the bottom of the stairs he stopped and waved his hand dismissively. "This is supposed to be a games room, but I don't play any games. Maybe I should get a pool table or something."

"How about Ping Pong?" Genie suggested. The large bare room looked almost big enough for a tennis court.

"Good idea," Byron agreed. He opened the doors to two small bedrooms, decorated in a tasteful but impersonal style. "Guest rooms," he said. "They have their own baths, and—" he flung open another door "—there's this big whirlpool room, with a sauna. I use it once in a while. There's a little housekeeper's apartment at the end of the hall, but it isn't used. Mine comes in by the day. That's all there is on this level."

"Very nice," Genie said, thinking that Byron's interest in his house was rather minimal. Either that or he was stalling for time, too.

He turned and went back up the stairs, taking a different direction at the main level. "Kitchen and dining room," he said, walking rapidly through two austerely modern rooms and ending back in the living room near the stairway to the balcony. "My room and studio are upstairs," he said. He glanced quickly at Genie and tightened his grip on her hand as they started upward. It was as if, she thought, he was afraid she'd bolt and run.

Running was not an option Genie was seriously considering. Her knees felt too rubbery. She clung to Byron's hand and tried not to think at all.

"This is my studio," Byron said, opening another door and leading Genie through it as huge overhead lights flashed on. "I took out a wall between two bedrooms and added a skylight. The fluorescents are broad-spectrum lights that mimic real sunlight, so I can work any time of the night, too.''

"I like this room," Genie said immediately. There was a warmth here, a clutter of living and working, that was missing from the rest of the house. Most of all, the room spoke of Byron's presence, from the paintings leaning against the walls to the cot he had mentioned, even a small table with a dry, abandoned sandwich on a paper plate. This was obviously the heart of the house, the place where Byron lived and worked.

In the very center of the room was a large easel, a table covered with art supplies close by. On the easel, covered, was apparently the canvas that Byron was working on. "Is that the painting?" she asked, gesturing toward it.

Byron nodded. "Yes," he said.

Genie looked up at him. His face was tense as he looked toward the canvas. He looked down at her and smiled crookedly. "I'm not usually this anxious about showing my work to someone," he said, "but I care a great deal about what you think of this particular painting." He led her to a spot facing the easel from about ten feet away. "Stand right here," he said, then dropped her hand and walked briskly to the easel. He took hold of the cloth, then glanced back at Genie. "Ready?"

"Yes. Yes, I'm ready," Genie replied, smiling encouragingly at him, unsure of what to expect. Her heart was beating rapidly, not from her own anxiety now, but in sympathy with Byron's. This was what had made Byron tense, not any concern about what might happen later. His whole heart and soul were involved in his painting, something she knew she might have guessed from his description of how completely it possessed him while he was working on it.

Standing motionless, she watched as he carefully removed the covering, then caught her breath, feeling her cheeks grow warm as she did so. "Ooh," she breathed, as her mind caught up with her soaring emotions. The swirling, intertwined forms on the canvas, one light and one dark, were unmistakably two people in each other's arms, making love. She looked at Byron and then back at the painting, completely in awe of the skill that enabled him to express so much in such simple, dramatic strokes.

"I've done it," Byron said triumphantly, his face aglow as he moved toward her. "You see what I wanted you to see." He caught her face between his hands. "I don't give a damn what anyone else sees, as long as you understand."

"But... how could anyone not see it?" Genie asked, bewildered.

"Easily." Byron shrugged, sliding his arms around her and looking toward the painting. "The critics get all wound up in their own interpretations. I can imagine some of them calling it an allegorical expression about the forces of good and evil, since one form is light and the other dark. But it isn't. Unless, of course, you're good and I'm evil."

"Not likely," Genie said, shaking her head, still stunned by the remarkable work. When Byron pulled her closer, she leaned her head against his chest and continued to look at it, dazedly drinking in the sensations of the warmth of his arms and the hard strength of his body next to hers, which seemed to come from both sources at once. He had come home last Saturday night, after he left her, and begun that painting, she thought. He hadn't forgotten her, those days he didn't call. She had been even closer to him than she would have been in reality. Her arms went around him and she sighed deeply.

"What are you thinking?" Byron asked, rubbing his cheek against her hair. "Does it shock you?"

"No, not at all. I was thinking what happened before you came home and started it."

"You think that I was working out my frustrations?"

"I don't know," Genie said, raising her head to look at him. "Were you?"

"Maybe," he replied with a smile. "Or maybe I was making them worse. And at the same time I was neglecting you." He lifted her hair and tucked his hand behind her neck. "I'm an odd duck, Genie," he said. "There's no getting around it."

Odd? Maybe, Genie thought, staring into the intense darkness of his eyes. There were visions there that ordinary men did not see, but he had shared this one with her in a way that she had never imagined could happen to her. It made her feel humble and at the same time elated, as if somehow she meant something very special to him that he could express in no other way. No other way, unless he were to kiss her. He was looking at her so seriously, as if not quite sure whether he should. Was he afraid, or did he think she was? She wasn't. Every fiber of her being seemed poised, waiting for the magic touch of his lips against hers. Slowly she raised one hand and slid it behind his neck, then gave a gentle pull to bring him closer.

With a groan, Byron crushed her to him while his mouth took possession of hers with an explosion of passion. Nothing that Genie had ever experienced before had prepared her for the intensity of her own response. It seemed that every nerve in her body was shooting off sparks of fire while at the same time she could feel everything with a brilliance that sent her mind reeling in a confusion of delights. There was the warm, moist softness of Byron's mouth, first devouring hers and then accepting her own eager explorations. There was a sensation of melting ever closer into his body, pressed close by arms that were both strong and gentle. His hair felt soft against one of her hands, his back hard against the other. A musky scent filled her nostrils and mingled with a sweet taste of honey on her tongue.

"Oh, Genie, I want you so," Byron murmured, his lips finding a new sensitive spot below her ear. "Let's go to my room." He swept Genie up into his arms, his cheek against hers as he carried her out of his studio and into the next room. He turned on a band of concealed lights near the ceiling and then dimmed them to a soft glow before he carried her to the huge bed, dominated by an arching headboard of oak. With one hand he swept aside the red-and-gold spread before he sat down with Genie in his arms and found her lips with his once again.

Moments later, they were lying down, locked in each other's arms. Genie reveled in the massive strength that seemed to flow into her body from Byron's. She felt as if her arms had grown strong enough to hold Byron so tightly that he would be a part of her forever. While their tongues moved together in an intimate dance of delights, he relinquished his powerful hold and pulled her blouse free, his hands delicately exploring the silken skin of her back. His gentle touch sent even stronger messages through her, messages of longing and desire that overwhelmed her frail attempts at conscious thought and left her floating in a sea of ecstatic sensations. When he unfastened her bra and slipped one hand between their yearning bodies to caress her breasts, she sighed softly. She wanted him to go further and further, come closer and closer. She felt as if they were flying into a strange new world of endless space, caught in a cloud of shimmering cosmic dust, and that if they kept flying together long enough she would never return to the world she had left. The clothing between them became an unpleasant barrier, and she blindly fumbled with the buttons on Byron's shirt, at last able to feel the roughness of his chest against her burning skin. He laughed softly and rolled her over and over. Together they tossed back and forth, murmuring sounds of pleasure, caressing and kissing, lost in a dream. Then, suddenly, Byron pinned Genie beneath him, his hands on her shoulders, his head raised above hers.

"We'd better slow down and think a little," he said hoarsely, his eyes so dark and deeply warm that Genie felt lost in their beautiful depths.

"What about?" she whispered, bewildered at the worried lines she saw beneath a lock of hair that had fallen forward across his brow. She did not want to think, she only wanted to go on with her beautiful dream.

"About what might happen if we go on," Byron said seriously. "Something I'm sure we're not ready for."

"Not ready for?" Genie said, confused. "I don't understand."

Byron sighed and smiled wryly. "I guess I'll have to spell it out for you. I doubt you're on birth-control pills, and I don't have any protection handy. I didn't plan...I'm not a swinger, as I said...and I didn't think to stop..." He lowered himself to lie next to Genie, still holding her close. "Are you angry?" he asked, as Genie stared at him dazedly.

"N-no," she said. Suddenly her eyes filled with tears and she buried her face against his neck. She had done it again. From the moment he kissed her at Portia's house, she had been his for the asking, her usually sturdy defenses reduced to some minor qualms that were easily overcome. But this time, she wasn't sorry or embarrassed, at least not for herself. She was only sorry that she had led Byron to a state of frustration that must be even greater than her own. What if he hadn't stopped? Would she have been sorry then? She wasn't sure. A strangled noise, half laugh and half sob, escaped her throat.

"Genie, I'm sorry," Byron said, his voice deep with anguish. "Believe me, if I'd known, if I'd had any sense..."

"I'm not c-crying because I'm sad," Genie choked out. "I'm glad someone has some sense, because I certainly don't. You seem to knock it right out of me." She drew back and smiled through her tears, gently brushing back the dark locks that fell across Byron's cheek. What a dear, sweet, beautiful face he had, she thought. She couldn't bear to see him looking so worried and unhappy. "I'm all right, really," she said. "I'm fine." Except that she knew, from the bursting happiness that bloomed in her heart when at last he smiled, that he had taken something from her this night, if not her virtue. Her heart belonged to this gentle, passionate genius who could touch her emotions in so many ways.

Byron shook his head and sighed. "We'll have to plan a little further ahead in the future. I guess I'd better spend the night on the cot in my studio. Unless, of course, you'd rather I take you home." He looked unhappy again.

"Anything's better than that," Genie said, raising her hand to caress his cheek. "I'm so tired of being alone."

Byron's smile returned. He dropped a quick kiss on her forehead. "So am I," he said. Then he quickly released her and sat up. "At least we won't be far apart. We can have breakfast together in the morning. Tomorrow I'm going to make a trip to the drugstore so I won't be caught unprepared again. Now I'd better get out of here or all of my good intentions will be for naught. Is there anything you need?"

Genie shook her head as she got up and straightened her clothes. "No, nothing, except maybe a little more strength of character. I promise—at least I'll try very hard—not to lead you on like that again until—" She stopped, feeling flustered, and gave Byron a sideways glance.

"What are you trying to tell me?" Byron asked, cocking his head and raising a questioning eyebrow. "That you wish I'd go to the drugstore right now?"

"Oh, no!" Genie said quickly. That wasn't what she had meant at all. But exactly what did she mean? She struggled to find the right words, while Byron looked at her questioningly. "I meant . . . I meant that I really don't think we should—" She stopped again and looked down and bit her lip. After the way she had behaved, how could she tell Byron that she would prefer not to have sex until they were sure about everything in their future? Or he was as sure as she was? Especially since that thought seemed to vanish from her head the moment he kissed her?

Byron came around the bed and stood in front of her. "Genie, look at me," he said. When she slowly raised her eyes to his, he studied her thoughtfully for a moment. "You're not trying to tell me that you can hardly wait until we get some method of birth control, are you."

It was a statement, not a question, but Genie shook her head vigorously, anyway.

"I see," Byron said, rubbing his chin and frowning. "Then what you're telling me is that you don't want to have sex with me until you're sure where, uh, all this is going to lead?"

Genie nodded. "Something like that," she said, wishing that she hadn't brought up the subject at all, instead calling on some heretofore missing inner strength to keep Byron at bay. Byron's frown was beginning to have a decidedly angry quality, the warmth of his eyes cooling rapidly.

"Something like that?" he repeated, his voice tinged with irony. "That's rather difficult to interpret."

"I know it doesn't make sense, after . . . after what I did tonight," Genie said, now feeling desperately unhappy at the hurt and confusion she read in Byron's eyes, hiding behind the curtain of anger. "I haven't any excuse. Maybe stupidity."

"That doesn't ring a bell," Byron said, tilting his head back and looking at her critically. "I haven't found that you're stupid about anything else." When a single tear welled over and trickled down Genie's cheek he scowled darkly. "Don't go to pieces on me, Genie. I am trying to understand. A better explanation would be more helpful."

"But I haven't got a really good one," Genie said unhappily, brushing another tear from her cheek. "I was brought up to believe that sex outside of marriage was wrong, but I'm not sure I really believe that anymore. I'm twenty-seven years old now, and it seems . . . kind of silly. And . . . when you kiss me . . . I don't care at all. But afterward, I still don't feel quite right about it. I don't know how I'd feel if—" She stopped, flushed with embarrassment at confessing her naiveté, especially in view of the skeptical look Byron was giving her.

"You're telling me you've never had sex with a man?" he said.

Genie nodded and looked down at the floor, wishing again that she'd had the sense to keep her mouth shut. Byron was silent for so long that at last she looked up at him timidly. To her relief, his expression was now more perplexed than anything else, as if he didn't know what to do with this freak standing before him. "Do you want me to go home now?" she asked in a small voice.

"Of course not," Byron said quickly. He smiled ruefully. "To be perfectly honest, I didn't think there were any twenty-seven-year-old virgins left in Southern California."

"Maybe you should have me bronzed and put in a museum," Genie said, making a wry face. "I feel like a freak."

Byron grinned. "Don't. I don't think you'll be suffering from your problem much longer. Meanwhile—" his eyes took on a devilish sparkle "—I'll try to be on my best behavior."

He left the room, leaving Genie staring after him, wondering if he meant what he said in his last statement or if that imp of mischief in his eyes implied the opposite. If it was the latter, she was in a world of trouble, she mused, slowly removing her clothing. She not only was putty in his hands, but her resolve to maintain her pristine condition was pretty shaky, too. He was just in the next room, and already she missed him.

Leaving on her underthings, Genie climbed into Byron's big bed and burrowed under the covers. Byron had been there and the scent of his presence filled her nostrils. She clutched his pillow to her and closed her eyes. "Oh, Byron," she whispered, "how I wish you were really here. I love you so much."

THE NEXT TIME she opened her eyes, it was to the sound of Byron's voice. "Wake up, sleepyhead," he said.

Genie looked at him and blinked. He was standing beside the bed wearing a dark red robe, holding a tray containing two cups, a carafe of steaming coffee and a plate of sweet rolls.

"I must have been dead to the world," she said sleepily, sitting up, the sheet clutched against her. "I didn't even hear you come in." She shook her hair back from her face and looked around for her tote bag. It was nowhere to be seen. "I thought I brought a little straw bag with me," she said, frowning. "It has my robe in it."

"It's in my studio," Byron said.

When he did not offer to get it for her, Genie noticed that the mischievous twinkle was still in his eyes this morning. Her confession had obviously been only a challenge to him. It even looked as if he planned on having breakfast in bed with her. She had better wake up and get her act together. "Would you mind getting it for me?" she asked stiffly, ignoring the grin that came to his face at her reproving look.

"Not at all," he said agreeably, putting the tray down on the nightstand. He bent and gave her upturned face a quick kiss. "Be right back," he said.

Genie watched him walk briskly from the room, her mind and body already a turmoil of mixed emotions. She ached to be in his arms again. There was no denying that she wanted to make love to him, even though the thought still made her anxious. If only she could be sure that he had more than sex in mind. Maybe then . . . She heard his footsteps returning and her pulse quickened. There was one thing, she thought, of which she was very certain. It was the love she felt as she watched Byron come through the door, drinking in with her eyes everything about him, from his dark, shining hair to his muscular calves and bare feet revealed below his robe.

"Here you are," he said, handing her the tote bag.

"Thank you," Genie said. She reached into it and took out her robe. "Turn your back," she said primly. "And don't look at me like that," she added as his devilish grin returned.

"I can't help it," he said, turning around as requested. "You're so completely adorable."

"Flattery will get you nowhere," Genie said, quickly standing up and slipping into her robe. "All right, I'm decent."

Byron turned around and looked her up and down. "I hate to tell you this," he said, "but with my imagination, you might as well be stark naked. However, as long as you feel safer that way, I won't complain. Prop your pillows up and get comfortable. We're having breakfast in bed." He set the tray in the middle of the bed, then moved to the side opposite the nightstand and got on the bed himself. He propped his pillows against the headboard and sat back with a contented sigh. "Sit down and relax," he said to Genie, who was still standing by the bed, vacillating over whether to do as he asked. "I'm not going to attack you. You can hit me with the coffeepot if I try anything."

Genie reluctantly sat down on the mattress and leaned back, turning her head just enough to look at Byron out of the corner of her eye. If he thought she looked adorable, she thought grimly, he ought to see how devastatingly handsome and desirable he looked to her. Her hands positively itched to touch him.

"That's better," he said. "Now look at me and smile. I'm not an ogre. And then pour us some coffee." His smile was so infectious that Genie couldn't help returning it before she sat forward and filled their cups.

Byron picked up his cup and took a swallow, then sighed contentedly. "This," he said, "is the way to start a day. I haven't had breakfast in bed in years."

"Neither have I," Genie said. "In fact, I don't think I ever have had just for fun. It was always because I was sick."

"That's a terrible state of affairs," Byron said, frowning. "We'll have to do this often. I think it's much better for both mind and body to ease into the day instead of jumping out of bed and immediately starting to rush around, worrying about all of the things you have to get done.''

"I never thought about that," Genie said. "My parents always pop out of bed when the alarm goes off and start right in. They both keep lists of what they have to do, and cross things off when they're done. My father hates to have anything left on his list when the day is over."

"What about you?" Byron asked. "Do you keep lists?"

Genie shook her head. "Not like that. Of course, I have to keep a schedule for my students, and I do sometimes write down things that I have to do and keep forgetting because I don't want to do them."

"Like what things?"

"Going to the dentist," Genie replied. She took a bite of a sugary roll and grimaced. "Like this is reminding me that I'd better make an appointment pretty soon. I think I may have a cavity."

"I wish you hadn't reminded me," Byron said. "I'd better get my teeth looked at, too. Funny how people hate going to the dentist, isn't it?"

For over an hour they stayed on Byron's bed and talked, beginning to explore each other's views on dozens of topics they had never had time for before. Byron made no suggestive moves or comments, and as Genie's anxieties about the situation vanished, she found herself thinking more than once that Byron's idea of having breakfast in bed was wonderful. Perhaps, she thought, the aura of intimacy made it easier to say things deeply felt. Whatever the answer, it was one more example of how very special Byron was, another reason to love him.

At last he tipped the coffee carafe upside down and shook his head. "All gone. I suppose that means we'd better get dressed and face the day."

"I expect so," Genie sighed. "Ms. Kitty probably thinks I've abandoned her."

Byron nodded. "Duty calls. I'll shower first and get out of your way." He took fresh clothing from his dresser drawers and closet and went into the bathroom, whistling softly to himself.

While she waited, Genie went to look out the window. The trees on the mountainside were bending back and forth in a dance to the winds that blew across the mountaintop. Dancers with no feet, going nowhere, Genie thought, staring at their hypnotic movements. Was that what she was, with Byron? It all seemed so unreal—her own dance at Portia's party, the night at Byron's house, this morning. Nothing like it had ever happened to her before. Byron had seemed content with her this morning. He had wanted her to stay even after she had told him of her reluctance to carry their physical relationship further. At first she thought he had taken it as a challenge, now she wasn't so sure. He wasn't an easy man to read. *I guess,* she thought with a sigh, *all I can do is wait and see what happens next.* Wait, and hope that, unlike the dancing trees, her own dance would go somewhere.

After Genie had showered and dressed, she found Byron in his studio, rubbing his chin and staring thoughtfully at his painting.

"Still like it by daylight?" he asked, glancing at her briefly and then returning his attention to his work.

"I love it," she answered truthfully. "Why? Is something about it bothering you?"

"One little thing," he said. "Would you mind waiting downstairs? I'll only be a few minutes."

Genie nodded. "All right." She would have loved to see what Byron did, but could tell that he wanted to be alone. Probably, she thought as she descended the staircase, he never let anyone watch him work. Maybe someday, if she was very lucky, he might let her.

She wandered idly around the huge living room. Her eyes fell on a bookcase, only partly filled with books, the empty spaces taken up with framed photographs. There was a professional portrait of two handsome dark-haired people, obviously Byron's parents. Next to it was a group picture with the same couple and their entire brood. Byron had been about eighteen then, Genie guessed. He looked arrogantly aware of his good looks, but his brothers and sisters were equally attractive.

On the next shelf was a group of snapshots of the family, mostly of the children. In the center was an enlarged snapshot of a boy about Tim's age. Genie stared at it. Her heart did a little flip, then began to race. She picked the picture up with a trembling hand and examined it more closely. There was no denying her first impression. Except for the fact that Tim was darker than Byron, they could almost be twins. Certainly brothers.

Genie bit her lip, her mind racing as fast as her pulse. Could her earlier idea be right, after all? Did Byron suspect Tim was his son, or at least wonder if it was possible? Was that the personal business that had taken him to Mexico with his lawyer sister-in-law? It seemed unlikely. He'd only seen Tim once before that. His reaction to Tim last night had seemed affectionate, but normal. If he were investigating Tim's records, surely he'd say something to her. Or would he? The fact that she was Portia's sister and might be upset by the implications of that idea might inhibit him.

Genie shook her head and stared at the picture. If she had this picture in her house and then saw Tim, she would certainly think they were related. If she had *been* the person in the picture...

"Genie?"

At the sound of Byron's voice calling from upstairs, Genie put the picture down quickly. "What?" she called back.

"Come up and see if you approve," he answered.

"Coming." She dried her clammy palms against her skirt and then hurried up the stairs, trying to still her apprehension. She was probably wrong about how much those two little boys looked alike, anyway. Tim's face was rounder, his nose smaller. With Byron's artist's eye he probably saw other differences. And surely, if he thought Tim could be his lost son, she would have noticed something special in his reaction to Tim last night. But there had been nothing in his manner to suggest anything more than a warm and friendly man responding to a darling little boy.

Outside the door to Byron's studio, Genie paused for a moment, reminding herself that what she was about to see was really Byron's first love and he would not appreciate it if her mind appeared to be on something else. As she had anticipated, he watched her face closely as she came to stand beside him and look at his painting once more. She knew she had not disappointed him by the way he quickly smiled as she first stared at the painting and then at him, her eyes wide, in completely spontaneous amazement at the subtle yet dramatic difference she saw.

"How did you do that?" she asked incredulously. "It's marvelous." Somehow, with a few strokes, Byron had made it appear that blond and raven locks were intertwined in such a way that they seemed to be swirling together.

He rubbed his nose, his eyes sparkling with delight even though he looked almost shyly embarrassed at her praise.

"Magic?" he suggested.

"I think so," she agreed.

"Well, since you approve, I think I'll leave well enough alone," he said. "Part of the trick is knowing when to stop. Are you ready to go?"

"I guess so," Genie said, smiling up at him as he put his arm lightly around her shoulders and they started down the stairs. She really did not want to leave, now or ever, but knew it would be some time before such a thing happened, if it ever did. In a way, she appreciated the fact that Byron was now being very careful not to set off any sparks in the sexual tension that hung in the air between them, the way he had deliberately taken the lead in exploring other facets of their relationship. He seemed to understand and actually be trying to help her in her battle for self-control, not the kind of behavior most people expected from an artist. They were supposed to be wildly abandoned, while tennis pros had steely control. Somehow, she thought wryly, they had gotten their roles reversed.

The midday sun was bright as they started down the hill toward Genie's house. Byron was whistling to himself tunelessly.

"I can see why you said you had a tin ear," Genie teased. "I can't tell whether that's 'Yankee Doodle' or the 'Habeñera' from *Carmen*."

"Neither," Byron said, giving her an exaggeratedly hurt look. "It was—" He broke off and swore, bringing the Ferrari to a sudden stop some fifty feet short of the turn into Genie's driveway.

"What...?" Genie's question froze in the air as she looked at what Byron saw. "Oh, no!" she cried. "One of my babies!" She flung open the door and ran across the street to where the yellow kitten that Tim had called Monster lay, limp and lifeless by the side of the road. She picked it up and hugged it to her, tears streaming down her cheeks. "Poor little baby," she sobbed. "Poor tiny little thing."

She looked up as she felt Byron's arm go around her and hug her comfortingly. "How on earth do you suppose he got out? He was too little to climb the fence."

"I doubt if we'll ever know," he said sadly, running one finger gently down the soft little body. "Do you want to bury him?"

Genie nodded. "In the backyard. Near Mother's azaleas. Oh, Byron, how will I tell Tim? He wanted this one so much. He was hoping to take it home today if Portia had time to get a litter box for it."

"That'll be rough," Byron agreed soberly, "but we'll think of something to make it easier. Do you have a spade?"

"In the back of the carport," Genie said. She found a small box and then carried the kitten to the backyard, where she watched Byron prepare a little grave, then set the box carefully into it and mound the dirt back. The tightness in her throat was almost unbearable. "Just a cat," her mother would have said, but was there such a thing as "just" an anything? She turned quickly and walked blindly back toward the house. Byron caught up with her and put his arm around her again.

"I think I've seen the rest of them," he said.

Genie nodded. "I think so, too," she choked out. "We'll know as soon as I open the door." She took a deep breath and opened the door. Ms. Kitty stopped by her feet and looked up at her, mewing piteously. "Oh, God, you poor darling," Genie said, tears beginning again as she picked her up and buried her face in the cat's soft fur. "You know, don't you? Your baby's gone." She heard Byron inhale sharply and looked up. Her heart almost stopped at the sight of his tear-filled eyes and the look of deep sorrow on his face. "Oh, Byron," she said, reaching out to touch his arm, "I'm so sorry. I didn't mean ... to remind you like that."

"That's not it," Byron said, shaking his head. "I can't bear to see you hurt. That's all." He smiled crookedly. "You'd better put Ms. Kitty down. You're getting her all wet."

Was that really all? Genie wondered as she set Ms. Kitty on the floor and watched her five other kittens gather around her. That was hard to believe. Losing a kitten was hard enough. How could anyone bear to lose his child, as Byron had?

"This gray one's a beauty. Do you think Tim would accept a substitute?" Byron said, crouching beside the group.

"I hope so," Genie said, her heart aching anew at the thought of telling the little boy that his favorite was dead.

"I might be able to persuade him," Byron said. "Do you mind if I try?"

"Mind? Heavens no," Genie said quickly. "I'll be happy if you can. I'd probably cry and make it worse for him. Let's leave the cats in the house so nothing else can go wrong while we're gone."

"I wonder," Byron said thoughtfully, holding the gray kitten up in front of him, "if it might be a good idea to take this fellow along. We could stop on the way and get a litter box and some food. Then, if Tim's agreeable, we can produce everything right away and keep him from thinking too much about the yellow kitten."

"That's a good idea," Genie agreed. "We've got a cat carrier in the attic we could put him in. We used to have a cat that went berserk in the car. You couldn't hold her without getting clawed to bits."

"Where's the attic?" Byron asked.

"There's a ladder that lets down from the hall ceiling," Genie replied, leading the way through the living room. She pointed upward in the small hallway outside her bedroom and gave Byron a rueful smile. "This isn't a very big house. The attic's tiny. If you'll pull that down, I'll go and get the carrier. There isn't room for you to stand up there."

Byron shrugged and pulled the ladder handle. "In case you didn't notice, I'm not that caught up in my house, except for my studio. I bought it mostly for the location. At the time, I was thinking of becoming a permanent recluse."

There was a harsh edge to his voice, and Genie looked up at him quickly. Lines of tension had formed around his eyes, which had a shuttered, withdrawn look. He was remembering, she thought. He was trying valiantly to hide it, but she could tell. "I'm awfully glad you didn't," she said, wishing that there was something she could do to ease his pain.

"So am I," Byron agreed, his expression softening a little. He reached out and touched Genie's hair with his hand, then suddenly pulled her into his arms and held her close, his eyes searching hers intently, as if he sought the magic formula she longed to give him. Then his eyes drifted down to Genie's lips, and his own lips parted.

Yes, kiss me, Genie said silently. *That will help.* But instead, Byron only sighed heavily.

"Go get that carrier," he said.

Genie hurried up the ladder, tears pricking at her eyes once again. Apparently even the passion they shared was no help against the kind of sorrow Byron was feeling. Would there ever be something strong enough between them to at least dampen its effects? If not, there was little hope....

"Find it yet?" came Byron's voice from below.

"Yes. I'm dusting it off," Genie replied. She climbed back down and handed it down to him. "Here it is."

"Looks as if it will do the job," he said. He put it on the floor and placed the kitten inside. "Hang in there, little fellow," he said as the kitten protested. "Now, where's a good place to get what we need?"

BY THE TIME they reached the Donaldsons' house, Byron seemed to have regained the good humor he had been in before they discovered the poor kitten. Genie did her best to follow suit, even though she worried that he might become sad again, between seeing Tim, who was a living reminder of the loss he had suffered, and trying to help Tim accept the substitute gray kitten. Watching him closely had not helped her tension, either. He looked so incredibly handsome, his dark hair blowing in the wind of the open car, that her entire body felt as if it was about to catch fire and explode. When Byron put his arm around her as they walked up to Portia's door, she could have sworn that she felt real sparks flowing between them.

He paused before ringing the bell and smiled down at her. "Feeling all right now?" he asked.

The deep warmth of his eyes made the last of Genie's worries melt away. "I'm fine if you are," she replied, then gasped as Byron's mouth found hers in a brief but passionate kiss.

"My, don't you two look chipper," Portia remarked as she answered their ring a few moments later and discovered them smiling at each other. "Come on in. We're out by the pool, watching Tim cavort around. You should have brought your swim suits."

"I'd just as soon sit and watch," Genie said.

"I've got a suit in the trunk of my car," Byron said. "I'll get it." He returned moments later with a gym bag in hand and followed Portia's directions to a room where he could change.

"You don't look too perky," Genie remarked as she and Portia walked slowly through the house toward the pool.

"Not enough sleep and a tiny bit hung over," Portia said, rubbing her forehead and wincing. "Tim got up at seven and started agitating about that kitten."

"Oh, dear," Genie said with a sigh. She explained to Portia about the yellow kitten and Byron's plan to try to substitute the gray one.

"Maybe he can do it," Portia said. "Tim thinks he's pretty special. If I tried, he'd have a fit."

"It remains to be seen what luck I'll have," Byron replied, catching up with them. "We'll have some fun before I spring it on him."

Genie greeted Mark and then settled into a lounge chair to watch as Byron dived in and began tossing a ball back and forth with Tim, thinking what delightful torture it was to spend an afternoon watching Byron's beautifully muscled body slicing through the water in a scanty pair of swim trunks.

"He does know how to get along with children, doesn't he?" Mark said as Byron initiated a game of tag.

"He's the oldest of six," Genie said. She told Mark and Portia some of the things she'd learned about Byron's childhood. There was no point, she thought, in mentioning Byron's loss of his own baby son. If Byron wanted to bring that up, it was his prerogative. Watching him with Tim, she was struck again by their similarities, but there were differences, too. Tim's build was more wiry than Byron's had been when he was a child. He did not look as if he would be as solidly muscular as Byron when he was grown, and as straight as Tim's hair was, he was going to have a terrible time making it look as good as Byron's if he let it grow longer. Even soaking wet, Byron's hair fell into deep, natural waves.

At last the two got out of the pool and toweled off.

"Let's get dressed," Byron suggested. "There's something I want to talk to you about."

"What?" Tim asked, clutching Byron's hand and chugging off at his side.

"If we hear a howl we'll know it didn't work," Portia said dryly.

Genie turned and explained to Mark what Byron was about to attempt, then the three of them sat quietly, waiting for the result.

It was almost a half hour before Byron and Tim reappeared. Byron was holding Tim, and Tim was holding the gray kitten. Tim looked as if he had been crying, but his smile was bright. Seeing their faces side by side, Genie was again struck by their similarity. She glanced at Portia, wondering if she saw it, but Portia had on large dark glasses, and the rest of her face revealed nothing but pleasure.

"This is Serafina," Tim said, sliding out of Byron's arms and taking the kitten over to Portia for her inspection. "Byron used to have a gray cat just like him named Serafina."

"Serafina?" Portia asked, lowering her glasses and raising her eyebrows at Byron.

Byron grinned and shrugged. "Tim says it has to be Serafina," he said. "I don't suppose a cat will mind as long as he knows he's loved."

"I don't mind as long as he doesn't have kittens," Mark said dryly. "Let's see him, son. He looks like a fine cat."

"He is," Tim said seriously. "Look how bright his eyes are. Byron says that's a sure sign." He turned his head and beamed at Byron. "Tell them about the boat ride," he said. "And then, can I have that ride in your car?"

Genie laughed at Byron's sheepish look. "Looks like you had to pull a few tricks out of the bag," she said.

"I couldn't bear to see him so unhappy so I suggested a ride in a rented pirate ship. The car ride didn't come up until we went to get the kitten."

As he spoke, his eyes rested on Tim, a gentle half smile on his face. His expression was so loving that Genie felt an ache in her heart. Did he wonder if Tim could be his, or was he only thinking of what might have been? She glanced at Portia, and saw her eyes darting back and forth between Tim and Byron. Was she noticing the similarity now, too? If she was, what was she thinking? She didn't know about Byron's tragic loss. If Portia knew everything that she did, Genie thought, she might be wondering if her cosmic forces had had something else in mind besides bringing Genie and Byron together. Another, heavier pain filled Genie's heart. Portia and Mark would be heartbroken if Tim were taken from them now. As unhappy, maybe more, than she would be to find out that kismet had indeed decreed that Byron run into her car, not to find her, but to find his lost son.

CHAPTER SEVEN

IT WAS LATE EVENING when Genie and Byron finally left the Donaldsons' house, having stayed for pizza at Portia's insistence.

"As long as Byron doesn't mind, stay and keep Tim entertained," Portia had said to Genie. "I don't feel up to it today, and Tim seems to think he's got himself an adopted uncle."

"I don't think Byron will mind," Genie replied, watching him help Tim build an elaborate castle out of his colorful set of blocks. "I think Byron's adopted Tim, too."

Byron had devoted most of his attention to Tim all afternoon, so much so that Genie began to feel vaguely resentful. She went outside and tried to read a magazine in the shade of a huge, colorful umbrella, but could not concentrate. Watching Byron and Tim together unsettled her. The way they smiled at each other, the way Tim seemed to like to be close to Byron, made her think that there was an almost mystical bond between them, and telling herself that she was getting to be too much like Portia, with her ridiculous belief in strange, unreal forces, did no good. She felt it even more strongly when she and Byron put Tim to bed. Tim insisted that Byron read him a bedtime story, and then clung to Byron's neck as if he couldn't bear to let him go. Byron's eyes were misty as he tucked the little boy's covers around him and kissed his round, tanned cheek.

"Sleep tight," he said huskily. "I'll see you next Sunday. You and I and Aunt Genie will have a fine cruise on that pirate ship. Take good care of Serafina."

"I will," Tim promised solemnly. "Very good."

Genie hoped that Byron would say something to her afterward to give her a clue about what he was thinking, but he did not. "A fine boy" was all that he said, and that to Portia and Mark as they took their leave.

When they were outside, Byron opened the passenger door of his car and looked questioningly at Genie, who shook her head. "I do believe this is where we part company. My car is still here," she said.

"Oh, yes. I'd forgotten," he said, smiling crookedly.

Just like you almost forgot I existed most of the day, Genie thought bitterly. "It's been a long day," she said with a shrug, trying for a lightness of tone that she did not feel. "Would you like to stop at my house for a drink or something?"

The conflicting emotions she saw on Byron's face made her spirits drop another notch. It did not make her feel much better when he nodded and said that he would. As she drove home, making no attempt to keep up with Byron's rather dazzling approach to driving in freeway traffic, she brooded about the day and then felt guilty for feeling jealous of a five-year-old boy, her own nephew. Why shouldn't Byron befriend him? It was remarkable that he could, considering the fact that Tim must continuously remind him of his own loss. She had no proof that Byron thought he was his son. All she really had proof of was the fact that Byron would make a wonderful father. If only someday she could see him giving such loving attention to their own children... But that was thinking much too far ahead. Right now, she needed to get herself into a better frame of mind, or Byron would be sorry he had agreed to come to her house.

Byron was waiting with the carport lights on when she arrived. "I think I know how the yellow kitten got out," he told her immediately. "When I got here, the door to the backyard was open and Ms. Kitty and all of the other kittens were in here. I think one of the neighborhood children might have gone in to play with the kittens and forgot to close the door."

"But the door was closed this morning," Genie said, frowning.

"Maybe he or she took the yellow one out and left it," Byron replied. "You'd better lock this door from now on."

"I certainly will," Genie agreed. "I don't want that to happen again. Your little calico might be next."

"I'm going to make her a house cat," Byron said as they went on into Genie's house. "I should have gotten a second litter box today. I'm afraid I was too intent on how I might make the substitution palatable for Tim to think of that."

"You did a wonderful job of it," Genie said, trying not to feel unhappy that Byron's mind was still on Tim.

"It wasn't as hard as I'd feared it might be," Byron said. "He's still young enough to be fairly easily distracted."

Genie nodded. "I suppose that's true. So, what would you like to drink? My father left some good Scotch behind, or there's brandy."

"Scotch sounds good. On the rocks," Byron replied. He pulled out one of the dining-room chairs and sprawled in it sideways to the table, waiting silently until Genie brought him his drink and then sat down opposite him. He took a sip of the Scotch and stared meditatively into his glass. "Good Scotch," he said after a few moments, then took another drink and flung his head back, his eyes closed.

Genie felt like screaming in frustration. Byron was obviously still a million miles away in his thoughts. She wanted him here, with her. She vaguely felt it was unreasonable, but the chilly fear that gripped her at the thought that Tim might be more important to him than she could ever be made her nerves as taut as bowstrings.

"Any cobwebs up there?" she asked snappishly when he opened his eyes and devoted his attention to staring at the ceiling.

Byron turned his head toward her. His eyes were narrowed thoughtfully and he seemed to be looking right through her as he answered, quite calmly, "I don't know. I was thinking how much Tim looks like my own son would have looked by now. Where was Tim born?"

That question, asked so matter-of-factly, sent a dizzying shock through Genie. Like fragments of a skyrocket, thoughts whirled through her mind. He hadn't thought of it before! What should she say? If she told him the truth he'd really wonder. He might ask Portia… No, he mustn't. She couldn't tell him. She wouldn't.

"In Los Angeles," she replied, keeping her voice firm and her eyes fixed on Byron's. "His mother was a very young teenager. She couldn't keep him. I think he's a very lucky little boy to have found such wonderful parents."

Byron looked down. At first, Genie could not tell whether she'd been convincing or not. Then he looked up, his eyes now so bright and intense that it took her breath away. He smiled at her. "He certainly is," he said. "Very lucky. And to have such an exceptional aunt, too." He finished his drink in one swallow and held out his glass. "How about just a little more? Your father has excellent taste in Scotch. What brand is it?"

"I—I don't know," Genie replied, feeling shaky with relief that she had diverted Byron and unnerved that his expression had changed so dramatically. "It's in a decanter."

"You'll have to ask him," Byron said. He got up and watched while Genie fixed his drink, then put his arm around her and steered her toward the sofa. "Come and sit beside me," he said. "I'm afraid I neglected you again today in my zeal to cheer up Tim."

"I didn't mind," Genie said quickly, not wanting to be reminded of her petty resentment now that she was getting her wish of having Byron's full attention. "I know Portia and Mark appreciated it, too."

"But I overdid it."

"I wouldn't say that," Genie muttered, avoiding his eyes as he sat down and looked at her across the rim of his glass. What difference did it make now, anyway?

"You didn't have to," he said. "I could read it in your eyes. I'm learning to believe them, instead of the things you say and do."

A little warning shiver went through Genie. Was Byron trying to tell her that he hadn't believed her story about Tim's birth? "Are you accusing me of lying?" she demanded, frowning at him.

"Good Lord, no," Byron replied. "I'm just trying to understand you. You're a very complicated person."

"I am?" Genie shook her head. "I've never thought I was. Why do you think I am?"

"Take that dance you did last night, for example," he said. "At first I thought that maybe I didn't know you at all, but now I understand. You thought I was up to no good. You were only trying to protect yourself against the threat of another loss. You're so sensitive and easily hurt. You feel very deeply for others, too, whether it's Ms. Kitty or Tim or anyone you care about."

"I suppose that's true," Genie said with a sigh. "Is that hard for you to get used to? I am trying to improve. When I got that costume and learned the dance, I was trying to be more positive instead of sitting home and feeling sorry for myself."

"Don't be too positive," Byron said, his warning modulated by a twinkle in his eyes. "I think we may be almost too much alike."

Alike? Genie frowned doubtfully. They might both be sensitive, but she had never thought she was much like Byron in other ways. He was brilliant and talented and rich and handsome. Of course, she did have some talent, and she wasn't poor, but...

Her eyes drifted down to his lips. It seemed like forever since he had kissed her. If only she dared. But here they were, on the sofa, and the way she felt it wouldn't take much to send her soaring out of control again. Darn it all, anyway. At least Byron didn't seem to be suffering from any great desire to kiss her. Darn that, too.

"I don't think we're all that much alike," she said sulkily.

Byron laughed. "I could tell that. I can also tell that you wish I'd stop analyzing things and kiss you."

"I do not!" Genie denied hotly. Maybe they *were* too much alike. She definitely did not care for his reading her mind as if she were an open book. "If you want to sit here and talk all night it's fine with me. What shall we talk about? The baseball season? I don't think we got to that this morning."

"I don't care much about baseball, and I don't think you do, either," Byron said with a knowing grin. "Why deny that you want me to kiss you? That's what I had in mind, too, when I brought you over to the sofa, but..." He caught her chin in his hand and studied her face carefully, then shook his head. "I don't think I'd better. I'm not sure I'm capable of restraining myself tonight, and I doubt you are, either."

"Maybe I'm getting tired of doing that," Genie said. Byron's eyes were glowing now with that soft warmth she loved to see, and she was getting anticipatory tingles from the way his lips parted slightly as his eyes dropped to study her lips.

"I hope not," Byron said slowly, tracing the line of her cheek with his finger, "because I've come to think that it's probably a good idea to hold off for a while. There are a lot of things to consider."

"What things?" Genie asked, her voice sounding thin and queer over the knot of tension that suddenly lodged in her throat.

"You've turned my world upside down, Genie," Byron replied. "Everything is suddenly different, and I'm having a little trouble getting used to it."

"You're still afraid?" Genie asked. She was no longer afraid of the risk, at least not when Byron was with her. He was, as Sondra had told her, very much worth it. Perhaps Byron was not yet sure that she was, she thought sadly.

"Don't look so unhappy," Byron said, squeezing her hand and then releasing it. "I'm not about to run away and cower in some dark corner. I'm having to adjust some of my priorities a bit, that's all. When I've got that under control, I think I'll be ready to forget all about the past and think about the future."

"I'm afraid I can't read your mind as well as you can read mine," Genie said, frowning. "I don't have any idea what you're talking about."

"That's just as well," Byron said soberly. "You might not like what you read." He gave Genie a quick brotherly kiss on the cheek and then stood up. "I think I'd better go now. I had an idea today for a painting, and I want to make some preliminary sketches before I forget it.''

''Does that mean you're about to go into a trance again for days and days?'' Genie asked, feeling frustrated and cross as she got up and followed Byron to the door. Her arms ached to hold him, and just when she'd about decided there was no point in staying a virgin any longer, he had decided that she should. If this was an example of cosmic forces at work, she was fed up with them.

''Maybe. I won't know until I see how things go,'' Byron replied. He stopped by the door and looked down at her, his eyes narrowed, his mouth in a grim line. ''I told you I'm an odd person, Genie,'' he said. ''Maybe you should think twice about how deeply you want to get involved with someone like me.''

''Maybe I should,'' she agreed, lifting her chin and giving him an icy look. She immediately regretted her thoughtless remark, for although Byron said nothing, his angry glare spoke volumes. Without another word, he jerked the door open and went out, slamming it behind him. Moments later she heard the Ferrari's tires screech as he took off up the hill.

Now I've done it, Genie thought, tears of frustration and anger filling her eyes. But he'd asked for that remark. No, she'd asked for him to say what he did, with her stupid comment about his going into a trance. She should have thought twice before she said that, but it had been such a strange day. It seemed as if almost all day Byron had been trying to back away from the passion they had felt last night. What was wrong? She wandered listlessly into the kitchen, picking up Byron's glass from the coffee table as she went by. He hadn't really wanted to stop in, she remembered. She could read him that well. Maybe it was because his new painting was already occupying his mind. But

he hadn't seemed to mind staying late at Portia's and playing with Tim until his bedtime. Tim again.

Genie sat down at the table and leaned disconsolately on
her elbows, staring into space, while questions with no answers darted back and forth in her mind. Did Byron really
believe her story about Tim's birth, or did he still suspect
Tim might be his son? As overwhelming as that loss had
been for him, still was, it would be hard for him to give up
that idea. Even if his mind told him no, his emotions might
make it persist. Did Byron really care about her, aside from
his obvious sexual desire? He had cared deeply about her
reaction to his painting, had said he didn't usually care that
much. That was a hopeful sign. But for most of the day he
had seemed to be trying to figure something out, as if he
was wondering exactly how deeply he wanted to be involved with her. He needed her, to be close to Tim . . .

That thought made Genie pound her fist on the table in
anger. She was getting absolutely paranoid! She was just
afraid. Afraid because now that she had fallen in love with
Byron, she would lose him, too. Not that she'd ever had
him. As far as she knew, he was still uncommitted. She
couldn't tell what he was thinking, and he was far more
complicated than she. The whole situation was complicated! If only she could talk to someone, but Portia was
definitely out. Maybe Sondra. She could trust her to keep
her secret fears to herself. In fact, Sondra would probably
just laugh at them. Well, maybe that was what she needed.
Tomorrow night she'd stop at Sondra's after she got
through at the club and talk to her. She doubted she'd hear
from Byron before then. He had looked very angry.

It was after seven the next evening when Genie knocked
on Sondra's balcony door, feeling even more frustrated and
unhappy than the previous night. The day had been marred
by broken appointments and a quarrelsome junior class as

well as her increasing tension over Byron's angry departure. What if she had made him so angry and disgusted with her that he didn't ever want to see her again? The worst part was that she wouldn't blame him a bit, the way she'd told him yes, no and maybe, and acted cross, jealous and unreasonable, besides.

"Are you busy?" she asked when Sondra opened the door, her face streaked with something that looked like tiny bits of colored straw. "I know I should have called first—"

"No, no, come on in," Sondra said quickly, standing aside so that Genie could enter. "I'm just trying to make some decorated flowerpots. What's up. You look sort of...desperate."

"I guess that's a fair description," Genie said. She pulled out a chair and sat down at the table, which was littered with tiny straw flowers and small pots, several already encrusted with an arrangement of flowers. "These are cute," she said, picking one up.

"But a pain to do," Sondra said. "Want a Coke or something?"

Genie shook her head. "No, just sit down and keep working. I need someone to tell me if I'm going crazy or not."

Sondra gave her a knowing glance as she sat down and picked up one of her pots. "Must have something to do with Byron de Stefano," she said. "Did he recover from seeing you do that dance the other night? He looked as if he didn't know whether to kill you or grab you and ravish you on the spot. You've certainly got him dancing to your tune. No pun intended," she added with a grin.

"No, I haven't," Genie said glumly. "I may have blown it completely last night. And then again—" she sighed heavily "—I don't know. It's so darned complicated."

"I'm all ears," Sondra said, deftly gluing a tiny dark red flower in place. "What's complicated? Trying to understand the great artist? I could have told you he's not like normal people."

"How did you know?"

Sondra shrugged. "I deal with artists all the time. They're weird. Work like fiends for a while, then go off on binges or take to the mountains and hike until they drop. Is that the problem?"

"Partly," Genie said. "I don't mind that part, really. But . . . can you keep a secret? This is really very, very secret."

"Of course I can." Sondra put down her work and pushed her dark hair back with the back of her hand. "What is it, Genie? Are you in some kind of trouble?"

"No. But there could be trouble. I don't know. You see . . ." Genie went on to describe her developing relationship with Byron and to recount everything she could remember about Byron's interest in Tim, from his first strangely intense expression on seeing him in her car the morning he ran into her, until his question the night before. "Am I crazy to think that he may really feel that Tim could be his son?" she concluded.

"Hmm." Sondra frowned thoughtfully. "No, I don't think you're wrong to wonder about that. He may very well have that in mind. You say he went to Mexico suddenly?"

"Yes," Genie said her, heart sinking. If Sondra thought the same way she did, she wasn't paranoid, after all. "But," she added, clutching at one hopeful straw, "that was before Portia's party. He'd only seen Tim once before."

Sondra sighed. "Yes, but if the resemblance between Tim and that picture of Byron is as striking as you say, that might have been enough to make him want to investigate any lead he could. And people with money can find out a lot, you know."

"I know." Genie bit her lip, feeling close to tears. "What shall I do, Sondra? I'm so worried for Portia and Mark, and I can't go on, wondering whether Byron's really interested in me, or if it's only Tim he cares about."

"Whoa, there," Sondra said sharply. "What was the second part of that statement? You wonder if he's only pretending to be interested in you so he can get close to Tim?"

Genie nodded and brushed a tear from her cheek.

"That," Sondra said firmly, "is ridiculous. I saw the way he looked at you at Portia's party. The man is head over heels in love with you. The issue of Tim's parentage complicates things, if it *is* an issue, but it doesn't change that for him, any more than it does for you, I'm sure."

"But it does, Sondra, don't you see?" Genie said tearfully. "I couldn't marry Byron if he was going to take Portia's child away from her. I just couldn't."

"You'd rather he took him and then married someone else?" Sondra asked, her eyebrows raised questioningly.

"Well, no. I guess not," Genie replied. "Oh, Sondra, it's such a mess. I keep thinking that maybe I'm imagining it all, but every time I almost have myself convinced of that, something else makes me change my mind again. What am I going to do?"

"The answer to that is obvious," Sondra said. "For your own peace of mind, if nothing else, you're eventually going to have to ask Byron about it. Don't rush into it, though. Wait until you can bring the subject up calmly."

"That's what I was afraid of," Genie said with a wry smile. "I just needed someone else to tell me. It's the 'being calm' part that's going to be the hardest."

Sondra grinned. "Here, take one of these magic flowerpots. That, together with whatever cosmic forces Portia has
conjured for you and Byron, should do the trick."

Genie took the little pot and looked at it skeptically. "I
don't believe in magic charms," she said, "but if it works
I'll give you a testimonial and they should sell like hot-
cakes."

Once at home, Genie set the little pot in the middle of her
table. "Make Byron appear," she suggested to it. Talking
to Sondra had made her feel somewhat better, but she
needed to see Byron and at least know that he hadn't decided she was too stupid and lacking in understanding to be
of interest to him anymore. She definitely doubted Sondra's belief that he was head over heels in love with her. At
the moment, she was too confused to even be sure how she
felt about him.

Two more days passed with no word. By Wednesday
night, Genie was feeling too depressed to eat. She cut up the
pieces of chicken from the microwave dinner she had
cooked and fed them to the cats. "I wonder if he still wants
you," she said to the calico kitten. "I'm going to advertise
the rest of your brothers and sisters in the newspaper next
weekend." She picked up the kitten and rubbed its chin
thoughtfully. "I could get a litter box and then take you up
to Byron. But if he's all involved in a painting he might not
like that. Maybe I should call. He said he wouldn't yell at
me if I did. But that was before..."

Genie put the kitten down and got determinedly to her
feet. She couldn't stand it anymore. She was going to call
Byron and talk to him. Right now! Where had she put that
card with his telephone number on it? Was it still in her
purse? She rummaged in the depths of her purse with no
luck. "Damn!" she said aloud. She couldn't have lost it.
She turned the purse upside down and dumped the con-

tents onto the table. There was still no sign of the card. In sheer frustration, she picked up her purse and hurled it across the room. It sailed all of the way to the front door, where it hit with a noise that sounded as if the door were being battered by a huge fist.

"My God, what have I done?" Genie cried, rushing toward the door, her heart pounding. How could her soft leather purse...?

It took her several moments to realize that someone was pounding on the outside of the door, someone who had started pounding at the exact moment her purse had hit it. Feeling almost weak with relief, Genie turned on the porch light and opened the door a crack to peek out.

"Byron!" she exclaimed, opening the door wider. "What happened to you?" If Byron had looked a little disreputable the first time she saw him, he looked even worse now. His paint-splotched shirt and jeans were the same, but his face was haggard and unshaven and his usually shining hair looked as if he had run paint-covered fingers through it many times. Burning in his pale face, his eyes looked like fiery coals. Uncertain of his intentions, Genie backed up a few steps, her heart pounding once again.

"*You* happened to me, that's what happened," Byron growled. He advanced toward Genie, flinging the door shut behind him with a bang. "I can't get a damned thing done. Stop backing away from me like a scared rabbit," he said in a softer voice. "I'm not going to hurt you." Genie stopped, trembling as he put his hands on her shoulders. "You're really afraid of me," he said incredulously.

"Y-you do look a little frightening," Genie said, trying to smile.

Byron glanced down at his clothing and then rubbed his stubble-covered chin. "Oh, Lord, I suppose I do," he said, shaking his head. "I'm sorry. I'd finally had all the frustration I could take and I jumped into my car and drove down here without thinking. Maybe I'd better go home and—"

"No! Don't go. I don't mind," Genie said, first smiling and then beginning to laugh. At Byron's mystified expression she tried to explain between peals of laughter. "It's funny. You came here...I was going to...I couldn't find...and then I threw my purse...it hit the door at the same time as you started banging on it. I thought my purse..." Genie dissolved into helpless giggles and threw her arms around Byron, burying her face against his shoulder.

"I'm still not sure I understand," Byron said softly, folding his arms around her, "but I do like this welcome a lot better. I wasn't sure what kind I'd get after the other night, but I had to find out. I couldn't bear the thought that you might actually hate me."

Genie raised her face to his with a happy sigh, drinking in the soft warmth she now saw in his eyes. "That's exactly the way I felt," she said. They were alike, after all. Even down to the exact time that their worries got the better of them. Or was it simply Portia's cosmic forces playing games with them again? Whatever it was, Genie didn't care, as long as she could feel Byron's arms around her.

"I couldn't get you out of my mind," Byron said, scanning her face as if seeing it for the first time. "I'd be trying to visualize something else, and all I'd see was you. I was beginning to wonder if you'd cast some kind of spell over me. And then—" he tucked his hand behind Genie's neck and began to lower his mouth toward hers "—I realized that you had."

The moment that Byron's mouth touched hers, Genie felt as if her entire body had turned into one of the fluid, swirling forms in one of his paintings. She melted against him, grasping him fiercely to her, reveling in the strength of his passionate embrace, the insistence of his thrusting tongue that darted along the soft inner surfaces of her lips. Even the roughness of his cheeks delighted her. The smell of paint, mingled with his own musky scent, was more wonderful than any perfume, because it was uniquely Byron. His hands spread wide along her back, then moved downward to press her against him. Genie made a soft sound of pleasure. She could tell how much he wanted her, and an answering surge of desire coursed through her. She wanted to feel his bare skin against hers, to be able to caress him without anything in the way. She slid her hand inside his sleeveless shirt and stroked his broad back. It felt like warm, silken steel, she thought wonderingly.

"Genie?" Byron murmured as he kissed his way along her jaw and then laid his rough cheek against hers.

"Mmm?"

"Put your arms around my neck and hold on tight," he said. When Genie complied, he lifted her into his arms and smiled at her dreamy expression. "I think I remember where your bedroom is," he said.

"I hope so," she said, leaning her head against his shoulder. "I'm not sure I do." She felt as if she were in some other world altogether, a world very far away from the one of anxiety and tension she had inhabited a short time ago.

Byron carried her into her room and placed her carefully on her bed, then lay down beside her and found her mouth with his once again while, with one hand, he deftly began to unfasten the buttons of her blouse. His movements were slow, as if he was taking great pleasure in slowly revealing her body to his eyes and his caressing hands. When he removed her lacy bra, he devoted his lips to stimulating the peaks of her breasts to hard arousal. Genie dug her fingers into his shoulders as he did, gasping in delight at the waves of desire his tender lips produced within her. She watched, heart pounding, as he crouched astride her and pulled down the soft flowered skirt she wore, revealing her little pink bikini panties and her long, slender thighs.

"Every woman should play tennis," he said, smiling at her as his hands stroked her legs from top to bottom and back again. "You have the most beautiful legs I've ever seen." He sat back, grasping his shirt and tearing it off over his head, uncovering his muscular chest with its dark sprinkling of hair. Then his hand went to his belt, pulling the tab free.

Genie's mouth suddenly became dry as dust. His touch had turned her body into one huge, hollow ache of longing, but seeing before her eyes what was about to happen sent a chill of fear through her. Was she really ready for this now? she wondered. And, if not, why not? Two minutes ago she had been. Why couldn't she just let herself go and enjoy her sensual side the way other women did? If only Byron hadn't stopped to take off his clothes...

Byron paused, his belt buckle unfastened, and frowned at her. "What's wrong, Genie?"

"N-nothing," she replied.

"Nothing?" Byron's eyes narrowed. "That's not true and you know it. What's the matter, don't you want to go on? I know we're still not equipped to prevent anything, but if you should get pregnant, I'll marry you immediately."

If she should get pregnant? The words echoed around and around in Genie's brain. What did he mean? That he wouldn't marry her if she didn't, or that he was thinking about marrying her eventually, anyhow? She was afraid to ask. And there was still the matter of Tim.... It took all of her wavering willpower, but at last she got the words out. "I don't think we'd better," she whispered.

Byron's head fell forward and his eyes closed. A few moments later, he raised his head, his mouth drawn tight and refastened his belt. Genie felt something close to terror. Had she, this time, really put an end to things? To her amazement, Byron looked up from fastening his belt and smiled crookedly at her.

"So tonight it's your turn," he said. "I honestly didn't come here to put you to the test again. I wanted to see you and touch you and know that you didn't hate me, but I meant to behave myself. Maybe it's because I didn't sleep at all last night." His eyes scanned Genie's half-naked body. "Put something on before I lose it again," he said gruffly.

Genie scrambled from the bed, shaky with relief, found her long terry robe in her closet and put it on. When she turned, Byron was stretched out on his side, watching her through drowsy, half-closed eyes that were still so intensely warm that she could feel their heat from across the room. As if they had forged a link between them, she automatically moved toward him when he held out his hand.

When she reached the bedside, he caught her hand and carried it to his lips, then turned it over and looked at her palm meditatively. "Such a strong little hand," he murmured, "to have tied me up in knots like it has." He rubbed her hand against his cheek, closed his eyes and yawned. "It's a good thing…you said…no," he mumbled through a second huge yawn. "When I'm this tired, I'm a lousy lover. I'd offer to go home so the neighbors won't see my car in your driveway but I'm not sure I'd make it. Maybe you'd let me sleep on your sofa?"

Genie shook her head and smiled down at him. Even with his rough stubble of beard and dark smudges of fatigue under his eyes, he looked so adorable and desirable that it made her heart melt. "Just stay right where you are," she said, "only get under the covers and I'll tuck you in."

"I was hoping you'd say that," Byron said, a little spark of mischief lighting his eyes briefly. He got up just long enough to unzip, then cast aside his jeans, before pulling the covers back and climbing into bed. "I don't suppose you'll get in here with me?" he asked, raising one eyebrow in Genie's direction.

"I don't think that would be a good idea," Genie replied, even though the idea had been tempting her from the minute she knew that Byron was going to stay there.

Byron made a face at her. "I knew you'd say that. Lie on top of the covers, then, and let me hold you. It'll give me pleasant dreams for a change."

Genie hesitated for a moment, then stretched out beside him.

"Turn your back," he ordered. "If I can see that beautiful face of yours, I won't want to close my eyes."

"I don't think you can help it," Genie said, but she did as he requested, snuggling close as Byron's arms came around her.

"Some exciting date I am," he murmured against her hair.

Genie smiled. Just having him here was exciting enough for her. "Go to sleep," she said. "We can talk in the morning."

Byron didn't answer. In only a few minutes, she could feel his arm around her relax. She slipped away, turned out the lights and went to curl up on the sofa beneath the old afghan her mother had crocheted so many years before. This, she thought, punching fiercely at the old sofa pillow, was getting ridiculous. This was positively the last time she was going to sleep in one room while Byron slept in another. The very last! It was time they got things out in the open. Apparently, Byron had had some thoughts of marriage, and she certainly had. It was time she gathered her courage and brought up the subject of Tim.

CHAPTER EIGHT

IT WAS GENIE who awoke first in the morning. She tiptoed into her room to get her clothes. Byron was lying stretched out on his stomach, his face turned toward her. His massive shoulders were bare, one arm bent and tucked beneath his pillow. With the dark stubble on his chin and jaw, his dark hair streaming back from his face, he looked, Genie thought with a wistful sigh, very much like a pirate. One whom, the stirrings within her said, she would have a very difficult time resisting this morning if he awoke and decided to make her his.

She smiled wryly to herself. Last night she had decided she wouldn't even try to resist again, but this morning the old reluctance was back. All the more reason to bring things to a head, one way or another, before one or both of them went berserk with frustration. She opened her closet and reached for a pair of jeans, but the jangling of the metal hangers made Byron stir. Perhaps, she thought, she ought to start the coffee before she got dressed. Byron needed all the sleep he could get. She started to tiptoe toward the door when a growly voice stopped her.

"Where are you going?"

Genie turned and looked at Byron. He had raised himself on one elbow and was watching her with a look of such raw desire that it ignited a shower of sparks within her. "I—I was going to start the coffee," she said haltingly.

"A good idea," he said, "but I have a better one." He beckoned to her with one finger.

Wondering if he had some magical power in that finger, Genie went to him. "What idea?" she asked, although it was plain from his expression what it was.

"Sit down," Byron said, patting the bed beside him. Genie sat and quickly found herself grasped and pulled into his arms. His mouth covered hers with a breathtaking kiss. Already soaring dizzily, she had started to knead his shoulders with her fingers when suddenly he flung himself away from her and sat up, his eyes almost wild with desire. "Damn it, I can't take this much longer, but we've been sensible this long and we'd damn well better keep it up a little longer," he said, throwing the covers back and getting to his feet. "I need a shower."

"I'll bring you some towels," Genie said, at first so stunned at the sight of Byron in only his briefs that it took her a while to get moving. If Byron thought he was tired of being sensible, he should feel how she felt! As she was getting the towels from the linen closet she heard a roar from the bathroom.

"My God, how could you stand to look at me? I need a razor, and shampoo!"

"They're in the bathroom," Genie called. She hurried to him with the towels and showed him where to find what he needed. "Anything else?" she asked, carefully keeping her eyes on his face.

Byron's eyes raked her slender body. "Don't ask," he said. "Go and make the coffee." He pushed her out the door and closed it firmly behind her.

"Oh, my," Genie murmured breathlessly. This was a new Byron de Stefano, his usual control stretched closer to the breaking point than she'd seen it before. She'd better get her clothes on before she made the coffee. With both of them hovering near the brink, it could be dangerous.

She quickly put on jeans and a baggy T-shirt, then glanced in her full-length mirror. That should do it, she thought, picking up a brush from her dresser and attacking her hair vigorously. To her eyes, she didn't look especially desirable, although that might not be the way she looked to Byron. He thought he looked terrible, while to her, it made no difference whether he was dressed beautifully or in rags, clean-shaven or not. He still looked wonderful. Maybe, she thought, that was what love did to a person. If so, it would be a good sign if Byron didn't think she looked less desirable in this outfit. Smiling to herself at her own perversity, she went into the kitchen and started the coffee.

She was just beginning the process of thawing out some frozen cinnamon rolls in the microwave when Byron appeared, clean-shaven, hair shining, with only a towel wrapped around him. The towel, Genie thought as she stared at him, was not the only thing he wore. His face wore a strong, dominant masculine look of pure sensuality.

"I can't put those filthy rags back on," he said as Genie gazed at his flat stomach and his long, bare legs and tried not to let the wild gyrating of her heart make her dizzy. "Did your father leave anything behind that I could borrow?"

"Well," Genie said slowly, trying to think of anything her father might have that would fit this magnificent male animal, "he's shorter and fatter than you are, but... I'll see." She went into her parents' room and rummaged through the dresser drawers. At the very bottom of one drawer she discovered a pair of bright Hawaiian swim trunks with an elastic waist that had been too flamboyant for her conservative father. "How about these?" she asked, holding them out to Byron, who had followed her.

"Perfect," he said. Without further ado, he dropped the towel and put them on, leaving Genie clutching at her parents' bedpost for support at the sight of his beautiful naked body. "Look all right?" he asked, tightening the drawstring around his slender waist and then tucking it inside.

"Better than all right," she said weakly.

Byron grinned. "You look a lot better than all right yourself," he said. "That shirt makes all those sweet curves of yours look mysterious and delectable."

Genie swallowed hard, dizzier than ever at the possible implications of that statement. "You're just too easy to please," she said tightly. "Come on. I think the coffee's ready." She tried to move past him, but he caught her and pulled her close against his side and walked along with her.

"Don't try to get away from me," he said, his mouth curved in a seductive smile. "I may not be able to keep my hands off you, but I'll be good if you will." As if to illustrate his point, he slid his hand up to just under her breasts and held it there.

"Stop that right now," Genie said, pushing his hand away, her cheeks burning as he laughed softly. She already wanted him more desperately now than she had last night and he probably knew it. But she couldn't give in now. She still wasn't sure of many things, and she had to go to work soon. If only she could hold out until then . . .

"Let's have breakfast on the deck," she said with sudden inspiration. It would be cooler and less dangerous out there.

"Good idea," Byron agreed. He helped her carry the coffee and rolls and orange juice to the outside table, then sat down and began devouring a cinnamon roll, his eyes, with their heavy-lidded, sleepily sensual look, never leaving Genie's face. Feeling completely unnerved, Genie tried to devote her attention to her own food, but her eyes, as if they had minds of their own that controlled the rest of her, kept straying back to Byron's broad, bare shoulders. He caught her looking at him and smiled slowly. "I suppose you have to teach today," he said.

"Yes," she replied quickly, glancing at her watch. "I have to leave in about forty-five minutes." *If I live that long,* she thought grimly. She felt as if she were slowly catching fire from the glow of Byron's eyes.

"I don't suppose you could take the day off."

Genie shook her head vigorously. "Not on such short notice. It wouldn't be fair to my pupils."

"What if you were sick?" Byron persisted.

"But I'm not," Genie said. "I'm perfectly fine."

"You certainly are," Byron agreed, with what Genie thought sounded like an almost lionlike purr in his voice.

"Byron, will you stop that!" she snapped, abruptly getting to her feet. "I know what's on your mind and you can just forget it!" Her nerves were drawing tighter and tighter, as if she were one of those tiny deerlike dik-diks she had seen on a television special, trying desperately to evade the pounce of a huge lion. "I think I'll leave for the club right now and give you some time to cool off."

She started for the door to go and get her purse, but Byron was upon her in an instant. He spun her around, picked her up and carried her, wriggling and twisting in his grasp, to the lounge. "Let me go," she said from between clenched teeth as he sat down with her in his arms and then leaned back, holding her against him with an iron grip.

"Not yet," he whispered, pinning her struggling body beneath him and covering her mouth with his.

For a moment she resisted, then her lips parted to receive his moist tongue, and she felt herself soaring into that magical land that Byron created with his touch. His hand crept beneath her shirt to catch each softly rounded breast and press the peak into swollen arousal. The frustrated longing, so close to the surface, burst through with a flood of desire that left her trembling.

"Don't," she said hoarsely, twisting her head away. "Please, Byron, don't torture me like this. I can't. Not yet."

Byron drew a deep, ragged breath. He pulled his head back and tucked his hand behind her neck. "I'm sorry," he said softly. "I'm just as tortured as you are, but that's no excuse." His eyes, slowly scanning her face, were so intensely warm that she seemed to *feel* their brightness. "Tonight?" he asked, raising his eyebrows questioningly. "If I get some protection?"

Oh, Lord, Genie thought, how she wished she could say yes. But she still needed to know exactly where they were going, and when, not to mention that she must know what Byron's role in Tim's future might be, a subject she definitely was not ready to bring up just yet. She shook her head. "I'm not ready yet, with or without protection," she said. "I need to know just where we stand first, and to understand . . . some things better than I do now." When Byron's expression darkened, she laid her hand alongside his cheek, tears coming to her eyes. "Please don't be angry with me," she whispered above the lump in her throat. "I know I must seem like a terrible fraud, leading you on like I have, but...I don't seem to be able to think very well with you near me."

"I know the feeling," Byron said grimly. He stared at her intently for a moment, then his face relaxed into more normal lines and he smiled crookedly. "I understand. We're very passionate people, you and I, but we can take a little more time to be sure of things, if that's what you want. But we'd better do it at arm's length, unless you like to be tortured.''

"I'm not sure I hate it all that much," Genie said, relieved that Byron was not angry.

"Neither do I," Byron said, his smile widening. He stroked her cheek thoughtfully. "When can you take a day off? I have a favorite place up in the mountains I'd like to show you."

"I don't work on Monday," Genie replied.

"Monday. I guess that would do. We're taking Tim on that boat ride Sunday. That should be fun. I've rented a sailboat and crew, and we'll sail over to Catalina and back."

"Tim will love that," Genie said. She was not too sure how she would feel, though. She had avoided the water since Kurt's death, but that was another fear she probably should deal with now. She pulled her hand from beneath Byron's shoulder and looked at her watch. "It's time for me to go."

Byron jumped quickly to his feet and helped her up. "I'll be here when you get back," he said. "We can go out to dinner someplace. I've gathered from looking in your refrigerator that you're not much of a cook."

"'Not much' is putting it generously," Genie said as she hurried inside to find her purse and keys. "I can scarcely boil water." She gestured toward the driveway. "You're going to have to back your car out so that I can get out."

Byron nodded. "I'll go on home and get some decent clothes if you'll give me your house keys so that I can get back in," he said as they went out the door together.

Genie handed him the keys. "There's something you could do for me if you wouldn't mind," she said. "I wrote out an advertisement for the kittens. It's by the telephone. I was going to call it in to the newspaper this morning, but I won't have time."

"I'll do it," Byron agreed. He bent and gave her a brotherly kiss on the forehead. "Don't work too hard. I may feel like dancing tonight."

"I'll be ready," Genie promised with a smile. She got into her car and drove off with a wave to Byron. What a night, she thought, and what a morning. She already felt like dancing, and singing a little, too. The events of the past twelve hours made her feel much more confident that Sondra was right, that Byron's interest in her was separate from any concerns he might have about Tim's history. "Mrs. Byron de Stefano," Genie said aloud and smiled to herself. It sounded wonderful. How soon, she wondered, would Byron feel ready to ask her to marry him, with no strings attached?

The morning passed very slowly. Genie was torn between elation and impatience for the day to end so she could be with Byron again. Portia and Tim stopped by at noon and insisted that Genie have lunch with them on the club terrace.

"Tim's so excited about the sailboat ride on Sunday that he can hardly stand it," Portia said, with a fond smile at her son. "I've told him that he has to be very good and do exactly what you and Byron tell him. It can be dangerous out there in deep water, with the riptides and all."

"Don't worry, we'll take good care of him," Genie said, suddenly feeling a pall descend on her previous good spirits. Portia would be devastated to lose Tim. She might find out soon if Byron really did harbor any notions that Tim was his lost son. Just what she would do if he did, she wasn't sure. It wouldn't change the way she felt about him, but it would definitely make things more complicated.

"I'm sure you will," Portia said with a sigh. "I'm just a worrier."

"I'm done, Mom," Tim said, pushing his plate away. "Can I go and play on the swings now?"

"Of course. Run along," Portia said. When he had gone, she leaned toward Genie. "You know, I didn't want to say anything in front of Tim, but it's really awfully nice of Byron to go to so much expense and time all because of that poor kitten. Of course, I suppose having lost his own little boy, he has a special feeling for children."

Genie's throat tightened. "How did you know about that?" she asked, trying to keep a calm expression.

"It came up last Sunday, don't you remember? Or was it when you were outside?" Portia said. "Tim asked Byron where he was born and then told him that he was born in Mexico and his parents were killed in the earthquake. Poor Byron looked as if he'd been hit by a lightning bolt for a minute. I expect it still hurts him to remember. Then he told Tim he'd been there when it happened, and he knew how bad it was because he'd lost his wife and baby boy that same day. They never did find the child, you know—" Portia stopped suddenly. "Oh, my," she said, her face turning pale.

"What is it?" Genie asked, although she knew only too well what had apparently only now occurred to Portia. Dear God, she thought, looking at her sister's distraught face, if only I could have spared her this. But there was nothing else she could have done, if Portia already had the facts Genie had so carefully kept from mentioning.

"It can't be," Portia whispered, shaking her head back and forth, "but why else would you two have met? It wasn't only for the two of you, was it? It was so that Byron could find his son! I'm going to lose my baby!"

"Portia, for heaven's sake, you're jumping to wild conclusions," Genie said, putting her arm around Portia and doing her best to sound calm and reasonable. "Tim isn't Byron's son. Byron left absolutely no stone unturned in the search. He told me how long he stayed, how widely he looked. Tim is your son, and that's that."

"But they look alike," Portia persisted, tears coming to her eyes. "They look so much alike. And you said his wife was Mexican."

"I think it's mostly their coloring and their dark eyes that make you think they look alike," Genie said, trying desperately to find some way to divert Portia. "Besides, if Byron thought Tim could be his son, I'm sure he would have told me, but he hasn't."

"He hasn't?" Portia said hopefully.

"No," Genie said. "You're just borrowing trouble."

"I suppose you're right," Portia said, looking somewhat relieved. She pursed her mouth and eyed Genie thoughtfully. "You might ask Byron sometime if he's ever thought about it. I mean, aside from just a passing notion. It's only logical it would occur to him, just as it did to me, isn't it? Unless, of course, he really is sure..."

"I'll do that," Genie promised. After all, she had already promised herself the same thing.

"Good," Portia said. "I don't know why, but just thinking about it makes me feel kind of funny and up in the air. I suppose it's because I still have to pinch myself sometimes to believe that we really have such a wonderful little boy. We knew so little about his background."

"I understand," Genie said. "I really do."

Later, on her way home, Genie tried to invent a scenario that would enable her to bring up the subject unobtrusively, but she had little success. She was, she realized, deeply in conflict between wanting to help Portia, and her

fears she might not help at all. She was sure now that Byron had been thinking about the possibility of Tim's being
his son when he asked her Sunday night about his birth. But
for the life of her, she could not understand why he asked
her, when he already knew, and why he didn't call her a liar
for the story she told him. Instead, he had seemed pleased
at her response.

A very complicated man, she thought with a sigh. Complicated and warm, and brilliant and sensitive. She didn't
understand him thoroughly yet. Maybe she never would.
But she didn't want to do anything to disturb their relationship, which was growing steadily into something more
wonderful every day. If a good opportunity came up to talk
about Tim, she would take it. Otherwise, she would wait
until Byron brought it up himself. He would certainly talk
to her before he said anything to Mark and Portia. And
what would she say to him, if he said he'd found out Tim
was his son and he wanted him back?

"Now look who's borrowing trouble," she muttered to
herself. She was getting herself all tied up in knots over
something that would in all probability never happen.

SHE STILL FELT on edge when she arrived at her house, but
one look at Byron, waiting for her in the elegant outfit he
had worn to the club party, and the subject began to fade
from her mind. When he swept her into his arms and kissed
her thoroughly, it vanished completely.

"You look gorgeous," she told him, when he let her
catch her breath. "I haven't anything to wear that looks
nearly good enough."

"Take off your clothes and go as a nymph," he suggested with a rakish grin.

"Are you planning to torture me this evening?" Genie
demanded, then burst into peals of laughter when Byron

said that he was and began to tickle her. "No fair," she gasped, trying in vain to find a spot where he was ticklish. "You're not ticklish at all."

They spent the first part of the evening at a restaurant overlooking the ocean, where the French owner greeted Byron like an old friend.

"Is the filet still perfect?" Byron asked him.

"But of course," the man replied, his eyes twinkling. "I do not want you to take your paintings away. They bring many people to see them."

"I told Gustav that I'd take them back if his quality ever slipped," Byron explained as Genie stared at him, mystified.

Genie soon saw what he meant, for the dazzlingly modern room, shining with mirrors and chrome, had several of Byron's paintings hung on the long, ebony-colored wall behind the bar.

"Does Gustav own them, or are they on loan?" she asked as they sipped a cocktail at a round mirrored table.

"He owns two of them," Byron replied. "I expect he'll buy the others as soon as he can afford to."

"I see," Genie said, suddenly reminded that the man she was with was a very important artist, whose works commanded almost astronomical prices. She smiled at him mischievously. "Could I make a small down payment on the painting you showed me last week? I should be able to pay for it by the time I'm a hundred or so."

"It's already yours," Byron said softly. "No one else could possibly have it."

Genie stared at him, tears springing to her eyes. "Oh, Byron," she whispered. "I—I don't know what to say. Thank you."

"That's quite enough," he answered, smiling.

The glow in his eyes was so deep and warm that Genie felt as if it had started an answering fire within her heart. She loved him so. He must care for her, too, to give her such a gift. If only he would say he loved her, she could cope with anything else.

They went on from dinner to dance at a small nightclub where an excellent combo specialized in Latin rhythms.

"Must be my ancestry," Byron explained, "but I can't get enough of Latin music."

Genie had never attempted a tango before, but Byron taught her the steps, and she was soon dipping and swooping with the rest of the crowd.

"This has been a marvelous evening," she told him as he delivered her to her doorstep. "I haven't had so much fun in years."

"That's what I wanted to hear you say." Byron kissed her lightly and sighed. "I think I'll go on home tonight," he said with a rueful smile. "I don't believe I could take another night of torture right now."

"I'm not sure I could, either," Genie replied, although she felt sad at the thought of spending the night alone. She bit her lip and stared at him. "Will I . . . will I see you tomorrow?"

"You'd better believe it," Byron said, kissing her cheek again. "If you'll give me your key again, I'll wake you up in the morning."

Genie unlocked the door and then handed him the key. "Good night, then," she said.

"Good night," Byron replied.

Genie watched him drive away, and then went inside. She felt as light as angel wings. Love, she mused, was indeed a wonderful thing.

IN THE MORNING, she awoke to the smell of bacon frying and discovered that Byron had taken over the kitchen and knew exactly what to do in one.

"Maybe I should learn to cook," Genie said, wondering if perhaps he was giving her a hint that she should if he was to consider her as a wife.

"It is a useful skill," he said, and Genie resolved to buy a good cookbook and begin to learn immediately. When she found that he already had a marvelous-smelling spaghetti sauce bubbling by the time she got home that evening, she was sure her earlier idea was right.

"I'm going to start taking cooking lessons right away," she announced. "This is embarrassing."

They had dinner, then watched television and talked until midnight, before Byron finally left, promising to waken Genie again in the morning. She slept so contentedly that this time she didn't awaken until Byron sat down on the bed beside her and bent to give her a kiss, which gave her the marvelous feeling that he hadn't been away at all.

"Ready for breakfast?" he asked, his arms stealing around her.

"Mmm-hmm," she murmured sleepily, clinging to him and stroking his hair. This was, she thought, absolutely the best way in the world to wake up. She felt Byron stretch out beside her. His arms tightened around her.

"Sure you have to work today?" he murmured against her lips. "We could have three whole days together if you don't. Three wonderful days."

Three days basking in the warmth of Byron's smile, going slightly mad in his tender embrace? It sounded heavenly. Genie dodged the soft lips that were tantalizing her face with myriad tiny kisses.

"Hand me the phone," she said. "I'll call in sick."

Byron let out a subdued whoop of triumph and handed her the phone. When she had finished her call, he gathered her close again. "Three days is much better than two," he said, rubbing his cheek against hers. "I think by the end of that time we'll have all our answers, don't you?"

Genie felt her heart do a skip and then start racing with a combination of hope and anxiety. What did Byron mean? Was he ready to declare his love and ask her to be his wife, or did he think she'd have a change of heart and agree to make love with him by then if he continued to shower her with attention and intimations of his affection? In any case, "all our answers" would mean for her that she must broach the subject of Tim, if he didn't bring it up himself. What would happen when she did, she had no idea, but she did know that the thought still terrified her. There were two very big questions to answer in three short days.

She lifted her eyes to Byron's and saw, in their dark centers, a longing as deep as her own. Suddenly, three days seemed a very long time.

"I didn't hear your answer," Byron reminded her softly.

"I'm sure we can," she said, sighing deeply.

"You're not sure," he said, tilting his head back and studying her seriously, a vertical frown line forming between his dark brows.

"Yes, I am," Genie replied, reaching up to erase the line with her fingertips. She might have been too timid many times in her life, but this time she would not be. Byron de Stefano was the man for her. She would not only find the answers she sought, but somehow she would make them be the answers she wanted. And, she thought, smiling as Byron's frown disappeared like magic, any help from Portia's cosmic forces would be greatly appreciated.

CHAPTER NINE

By SUNDAY, Genie was almost sure she was going to like the answer to her first question. Byron seemed to be drawing her deeper and deeper into his life. They spent Saturday afternoon at his house, where he showed her the rudiments of his painting technique and let her try it herself.

"Paint what you feel about something that you know very well," he told her, and then generously applauded her efforts to portray the morning mists creeping along the mountainside like gray and white kittens at play.

The kitten theme reminded Genie that she would not be home to receive answers to her advertisement for the kittens. When she mentioned the fact, Byron confessed shamefacedly that he had not placed the ad.

"I decided to keep them all myself," he said, looking very much like a small boy who had been caught stealing candy. "I've gotten used to having them around at your house. Besides, they'd miss each other's company."

"But, Byron," Genie said, both appalled and delighted by his confession, "pretty soon they'll be five big cats. You'll be overrun with cats. Litter boxes to change, cat hair to vacuum up."

"My housekeeper may as well earn her salary. She doesn't have much to do right now," he replied with a shrug. "If they get to be too much later on, we'll figure it out then."

His use of "we" set Genie's nerves to tingling. Did he mean we, as in the two of them, together, in his house? And if he did, why didn't he say so?

Sondra added to her tension when, that evening, they ventured out to a beach party thrown by a group of artists in Laguna Beach. "Has he popped the question yet?" she asked.

"No," Genie answered with a frown. "You know I'd have told you if he had."

Sondra grinned. "Then he's just about to," she said. "He looks at you as if he's already taken possession."

Genie glanced in the direction that Sondra was looking and saw Byron watching her, a proprietorial look on his face that clearly warned any other male to keep his distance. Was he on the verge of proposing marriage? If so, she had better bring up question number two very soon.

Later that night, as they sat snuggled together on the lounge on her deck, watching the stars, she tried desperately to find some way to bring up the subject of Tim's parentage without making it seem that she was accusing Byron of being either foolishly hopeful or thoughtless of Portia and Mark's love for their adopted son. Nothing came to mind. The attempt made her so jittery that Byron asked what was bothering her.

"I guess it's going on that sailboat ride tomorrow," she said to divert him. "I've avoided going out ever since Kurt died, even though I used to enjoy it a lot. But I've got to get over that. I'll be all right."

Byron accepted her explanation with a warm concern that made her feel guiltier than ever for lying to him.

"I never thought about that when I suggested the trip," he said soberly. "Is there anything I can do to make it easier for you?"

"Just be there," Genie said. "You make me feel safe."

"Not afraid anymore?" Byron asked.

From the deep, husky quality of his voice Genie could tell that his simple question meant more than its words revealed. Perhaps, she thought, that was one of the questions he had needed to answer. "No," she said softly. "Not anymore. Are you?"

Byron was silent for several moments. "Not about the future," he said at last, "and I think my problems from the past are just about laid to rest, too." When Genie became tense in his arms, he nuzzled her ear with his lips. "Don't worry about it, sweetheart," he said.

"I—I just wondered if I could help," she said hesitantly, while at the same time she wished fervently that if his problems involved Tim he would come right out and say so.

"No," he replied with a sigh, "it's something I have to take care of myself. I'll tell you about it as soon as I can."

Genie leaned her head away and looked at him. His expression was serious and withdrawn, almost sad. "They must be very difficult problems," she said, hoping to draw him out.

He smiled, the sadness disappearing. "Not really. When I'm holding you in my arms, they don't seem difficult at all."

"That," Genie said, wrinkling her nose at him, "is a very flattering but cryptic answer. Try again."

"I'm sorry," Byron said. "I shouldn't have said anything about it. I'd like to say more, but now isn't the time. It's getting late."

After he had gone, Genie tossed and turned, trying to figure out, with no success, what his difficult problem might be. It might involve Tim, or it might involve any number of things she knew nothing about. Or it might have something to do with asking her to marry him. Maybe, she thought wryly, it was related to the fact that she was to go to Byron's house in the morning and make her first attempt at cooking a real breakfast. Her whole future might hinge on whether she showed any aptitude for cooking!

In the morning, she was seriously in doubt that she did.

"I can't believe you've never even fried bacon," Byron said, shaking his head despairingly. "Didn't your mother try to teach you?"

"No. I played tennis, remember? Portia was the domestic one. She's a marvelous cook. But I can learn, if you don't frown at me like that," she added, mopping up a spot of grease that escaped the pan when she flopped a slice of bacon over with too much vigor.

Byron grinned but said nothing. She had just begun cooking some pancakes when the telephone rang.

"That's probably Elisa," Byron said. "I'll get it in the other room. Turn those when bubbles form in the middle."

Elisa. Genie frowned. That name brought back memories of a much unhappier day. Was that elegant lady lawyer somehow involved in Byron's continuing problems from the past? Perhaps still pursuing clues about Tim's parentage? Or was it something difficult, but more innocuous? A problem connected to Byron's late wife's estate. That could be quite complicated, with a proud and wealthy family involved, as well as money in two different countries. Yes, Genie decided, that was much more likely.

"Oops!" The pancake that Genie attempted to turn over landed halfway across another one. How did everyone else make this look so easy? Byron must think she was a real dunce. She managed to straighten it out, took out the first batch and started another. They were on their second side when Byron returned, his jaw set, his mouth in a grim line.

"Bad news?" she asked, a little shiver of anxiety running through her.

Byron shook his head. "Not really," he replied. He took a deep breath, forced a little smile and then peered critically at Genie's accumulating pile of pancakes. "Not bad," he said. "Some of them are even round."

"Thanks, I think," she said dryly. "Shall we see if they're edible in other shapes?"

Genie could see that Byron was still distracted by his telephone call, for he had little to say while they ate breakfast, seeming to have to rouse himself from deep thought each time he made a remark. If only he would tell her what was wrong. Wondering about it was going to make her a nervous wreck, too, and their sailing expedition would turn out to be less than the jolly outing they had planned. However, by the time they were ready to leave to pick up Tim, Byron had managed to shake off his mood, and Genie's spirits had risen as a result.

"Think I look enough like a pirate?" he asked, appearing in a T-shirt with horizontal red and white stripes, blue jeans and one of his red bandannas tied around his forehead.

"I'm sure Tim will think so," Genie replied.

"You don't?" Byron feigned a hurt look.

"Of course I do. You make me wish I had a period costume so I could look like a proper pirate's lady," she said. "Jeans and a T-shirt don't quite do it for me, I'm afraid."

"Ah, milady, they do it for me," Byron said with a rakish smile. "I am prepared to ravish you at the first opportunity. However, I'm afraid I dare not make unseemly advances in front of your nephew, so you are safe for the time being. But beware, for your time is running out."

"You make my poor little heart flutter," Genie said, batting her eyelashes. "I think we'd better hurry off. I don't feel safe here."

They drove Genie's car in order to have room for Tim, who was very disappointed to find he was not going to have another ride in Byron's car.

"I was afraid he was going to be sick, he's been so excited," Portia said to Genie as they followed Byron and Tim outside. She gave Genie a meaningful look. "Did you have a chance to ask him . . . anything?" she said softly.

Genie shook her head. "No, but don't worry about it. If it will make you feel better, I promise I'll ask tomorrow." Portia looked even more overwrought than Tim, her usually serene features puckered into anxious lines.

"I'm not sure it will," Portia replied. "I just have this funny feeling."

"Well, I don't," Genie said firmly, even though thinking about broaching the subject tomorrow made her stomach queasy. Well, it was a sort of deadline, and she had to get it over with, she told herself, forcing herself to smile brightly and add, "I recommend you take a brisk walk and then read something stimulating. You've gotten yourself into a state over nothing."

"You're probably right," Portia said, smiling weakly. "Well, have a good time. Tim, you behave yourself. It's pretty windy today. I don't want to hear that you fell overboard being silly."

"Don't worry," Byron said, smiling at her. "He'll have on a life jacket and I plan to tie a rope onto him besides. We pirates don't let our captives get away."

"Am I your captive?" Tim asked, wide-eyed.

"You bet," Byron replied. "I'll have you swabbing the deck before you know it."

For the rest of the afternoon, Genie felt like a spectator, watching Byron make Tim feel that he was on a real pirate's ship, even though the luxurious yacht he had chartered was far more suitable for royalty.

"Captured it from the Queen's navy," he explained when she remarked on it. He let Tim help steer the boat, tie her up when they stopped at Avalon on Catalina for a tour through some shops, then cast off again when they left. They docked again in Long Beach just before sunset.

"Have a good trip, mate?" Byron asked Tim, who was so tired that he was yawning mightily as they left the harbor.

"Real good," Tim said, "but I wish Mom and Dad could have come along. They never got to see a real pirate ship before."

"We'll do it again," Byron promised, "and next time bring the whole family."

"Even Serafina?" Tim asked.

"Even Serafina," Byron said.

Tim was sound asleep, clutching the brightly colored plush parrot Byron had bought him on Catalina, by the time they reached the Donaldsons' house. Byron carried him inside.

"One worn-out little sailor," he said to Portia. "Shall I carry him up to his bed?"

"Yes, of course," Portia said, following Byron as he started for the stairs.

Genie stayed behind to talk to Mark, who had signaled silently that he wanted her to stay.

"Have you any idea what's bothering Portia?" he asked. "She's been nervous as a cat the past few days. I can't believe it was all because Tim was going to be on a boat for a few hours, but that's what she said it was."

"I noticed it, too," Genie said, feeling guilty as she shook her head in the negative.

Mark shrugged. "Well, maybe she'll get over it now. Have a good time? That's your first time out since...since Kurt's accident, isn't it?"

"Yes. Yes it is," Genie replied, suddenly realizing that she hadn't even thought about that all day. "It didn't bother me at all. I thought it might, but it didn't."

"Good girl," Mark said approvingly. "I can't tell you how pleased I am that you and Byron have gotten together. He's a fine man. Of course, I figure that anyone who likes you and Tim is an excellent judge of character." He paused and chuckled. "Did I say likes? It's pretty obvious he does a lot more than *like* you."

Genie smiled but said nothing. It seemed obvious to her that Byron did a lot more than *like* Tim, too.

Byron declined Mark's invitation to stay for a drink, pleading that keeping up with a five-year-old had worn him out, too. He was silent as they drove back to Genie's house, seeming as lost in thought as he had been that morning. "Just tired," he said, when she asked why he was so quiet. When he parked her car and then sat and stared into space, Genie began to wonder if something very serious was wrong.

"Are you all right, Byron?" she asked.

He nodded, then finally turned to look at her. "I think I'll go on home," he said. "I need to make some plans for tomorrow. I'll call you when I'm coming to get you, but don't be surprised if it's after ten. I have some things to do first."

"All right," Genie said, trying not to look as disappointed as she felt. It was going to be a very long evening without Byron's company, especially in view of the questions that still remained unanswered. What were the mysterious plans he had for tomorrow? Were they related to his moodiness since Elisa's phone call? She walked to her door with Byron at her side, wondering if he was even going to kiss her good-night and not very surprised when she got only a perfunctory kiss on the lips. She was surprised at the way Byron held her, his grip almost crushing, for a long time saying nothing, softly rubbing his cheek against her hair.

"Good night, Genie," he said, at last releasing her. He tipped her chin up with his fingertips. "Did you have a good day?"

"Very good," she answered. "Did you?"

Byron smiled wryly. "One of my best, I think," he said. "One of my best."

Now what did he mean by that "I think"? Genie wondered, frowning as she watched him drive away. She was growing tired of his cryptic remarks. Tomorrow he was either going to tell her exactly what they all had meant or she was going to give him a large piece of her mind. She could excuse, even encourage, his withdrawing into uncommunicative silence when he was working on one of his magnificent paintings, but she was not going to put up with a lack of communication on a day-by-day basis. Odd man or not, he was going to talk to her. That was the only way for a husband and wife to get along year after year.

Genie stopped just inside her door and suddenly smiled to herself, then laughed out loud. Something had happened to her these past few weeks. Something amazing and quite wonderful. She was no longer the timid, frightened person she had often felt she was. Portia was leaning on her now. And she was so determined that Byron was going to be her husband that she doubted wild horses or all the cosmic forces in the universe could deter her. Maybe that was because she had never wanted anything so much before. She had loved Kurt and wanted to marry him because he gave her a strong shoulder to lean on. She had wanted to play tennis, because her father wanted it. But Byron... she wanted him because he was so very special, like her but different, adding a dimension of excitement and wonder and love to her life that no one else could possibly add. Maybe fate had brought him into her life, and Tim's, but she was taking charge now, because she knew what she wanted.

And what about Tim? a chilling little voice whispered inside of her. *What if Portia's premonitions, your own wonderings, are right? What will you do then?*

"I'll cross that bridge when I come to it," Genie murmured, clenching her hands as if to do battle with her shadowy opponent. Tomorrow she was going to get everything out in the open and deal with whatever she found. She could do it because she had to. She and Byron were meant to be together. She could feel it as strongly as if it were actually written in the stars.

Genie smiled wryly to herself and went to get ready for bed. Maybe Portia really did have something with her reliance on supernatural forces, and maybe she didn't, but it didn't hurt to have that kind of certainty. She might need all of it tomorrow.

CHAPTER TEN

GENIE AWOKE EARLY the next morning, unable to go back to sleep, her body already surging with the kind of nervous anticipation she had always felt before an important tennis match. She got up and dressed in jeans and a long-sleeved denim shirt. Byron had told her they would be hiking in an area where there might be some poison oak, and to be well covered, just in case. As she tied her long hair back in a ponytail she noticed in the mirror that her eyes were unusually bright, as if they were reflecting her heightened tension.

"Keep calm, Genie," she muttered as she spilled some of the coffee she was measuring into the filter basket. It was only a little after seven. She might have almost three hours to wait before Byron called. It occurred to her that it was a little odd that he had said he'd call instead of coming right down to her house. Oh, well, he probably had a reason. If she let every little thing bother her, she was going to be in a terrible state.

She sat at the table and drank her coffee, too excited to eat, trying to study one of her mother's cookbooks and begin to learn some of those long-neglected skills. A recipe for a devil's food cake caught her attention, and she vaguely wished she had the time and the ingredients to try it. But even if she had everything she needed, there wasn't enough time for a beginner like her, even though the clock was creeping along at a snail's pace. She put the cookbook away and began pacing back and forth.

"Damn, but I wish he'd call," she said, glancing at the kitchen clock as she passed it for what felt like the ten-thousandth time. It was only nine o'clock but it felt like noon. When the telephone rang five minutes later, she almost broke her toe tripping over a chair as she raced to answer it. "Hello," she gasped, trying to suppress the pain.

"Genie? You've got to come over right away!" It was Portia, sounding tear-choked and hysterical.

"Why? What's happened?" Genie asked, although a terrible fear suddenly gripped her and made her hands instantly clammy. Had Portia's premonitions become reality?

"I can't tell you on the phone," Portia sobbed. "Please come over right away."

Get hold of yourself, Genie told herself firmly as her instinctive desire to run to Portia's side surged through her. "I can't come right away," she said. "I'm expecting Byron any minute."

Portia let out a shriek. "Don't mention that man's name to me! If you knew what he's done you'd never want to see him again!"

"Oh, God," Genie said, feeling sick. Her worst fears, the ones she had tried so hard to ignore, had come true. What on earth should she do now? She wanted to comfort Portia, but she also wanted to know exactly what had happened before she confronted Byron. "Did Byron call you?" she asked.

"No. Some...some person from the agency. Mrs. Ramirez. Some lawyer's been snooping around, asking a lot of questions. Someone connected with Byron. She said there's been a mistake..." Portia's sobs overcame her and she paused.

"What else did she say?" Genie asked, her heart aching for her sister's anguish while at the same time she could feel Byron's joy and relief at finding his little boy.

"I couldn't understand her very well," Portia choked out between sobs. "She had such an accent." She stopped again. "Oh, Genie," she finally gasped, "I'm going to lose my baby."

"Hold on," Genie said, trying to sound calm while her own tears were beginning to fall. "All you heard was that there's been some mistake? That could mean a lot of things."

"What else could it mean?" Portia cried hysterically. "All it would take is a blood test to prove that Byron is Tim's father. I just know it."

"No, you don't," Genie said, although she felt almost as certain as Portia. She sighed heavily and dashed the tears from her cheeks. "Where's Mark?" she asked. "Does he know?"

"No," Portia moaned, "and he's gone to Bakersfield for a conference. He won't be back until tonight. Thank God Tim went with the Murphys to the beach so he didn't hear me start screaming. What will the poor baby think when he finds out?"

"Portia, for heaven's sake, don't say anything to him yet," Genie said seriously. "Not until you know the details."

"Of course not," Portia replied, her voice hurt. "Do you think I'm a fool? But you can see why I need you here, can't you? I can't face this alone all day. I'm going out of my mind with worry."

"I know," Genie said, feeling so torn that she felt as if her very body were being divided. "But you've got to understand something, Portia. I love Byron. I know how he must feel, too. It makes it...very hard for me to know what to do right now. I think I'd better talk to Byron right away.... Portia? Portia, are you there? Are you all right?" There was no answer for a moment, only a sort of gasping sound. Finally Portia's voice returned, harsh and angry.

"You love Byron? After what I've told you? You're no sister of mine!"

"Dear God," Genie said, staring at the receiver after hearing Portia bang down the one at her end. Portia was hysterical, she felt as if her own life were being shredded into bits, and she had no idea what she could do to make things better. She stared desolately into space for several minutes, her mind churning with images of Byron and Tim and Portia, desperately trying to make something logical emerge from the morass of despair. At last she sighed heavily. She could run to Portia's aid, but that wouldn't help the way she felt. She didn't want to listen to her sister tell her she couldn't love the man she loved. The only thing that she could do was to talk to Byron, right away. If he wasn't ready to talk to her, that was just too bad. It had to be done.

Genie went to her car and drove swiftly up the hill. She had only gotten a little way into the driveway when she stopped, her heart pounding even harder than it had been, her head spinning dizzily at what she saw. It couldn't be, but it was. A huge moving van was backed up to Byron's door, and men were carrying out his furniture. Byron's own car was nowhere in sight.

As if in a dream, Genie got out of her car and walked over to where one of the men was standing, mopping his brow.

"Is, uh, Mr. de Stefano here?" she asked, knowing he was not.

"No, ma'am," the man replied.

"Do you know where he is? Where he's moving to?" she asked.

The man shook his head. "We've got orders to move this stuff out and take it to our warehouse. That's all I know."

"Thank you," Genie whispered. She went back to her car, feeling completely numb. Byron had gone. He had run away. He couldn't face her with the truth, so he had run away. And from somewhere far away, he would reach out and take Tim away from Portia.

Feeling completely desolate, Genie drove back down the hill. She did not even glance at her parents' house as she passed. She had to get away, go somewhere where nothing reminded her of Byron, and think. She turned south on the Coast Highway and drove, unseeingly, for miles. At last she came to a small park, where a rocky promontory over-looked a deserted stretch of beach. Without consciously planning it, she parked her car and got out, only as she climbed onto the rocks remembering that this was the place she used to come to think when she was younger, before Kurt died and she began to shun the ocean. Here she had sat and cried over losing another tournament match, cried when her favorite cat died. But now, as she huddled on the rocks in the chilly ocean breeze, she could not cry. She could only think that she wanted to die, to make the terrible pain go away forever. She stared into the deep blue water at the base of the rocks. What would it be like to fall down there, maybe striking her head on the way, and sink slowly, inevitably, to the bottom? It wouldn't be so bad. Only a few moments of pain, and then endless sleep. It might be cowardly, but she was so tired. Tired of losing everything she loved.

She moved closer to the edge, started to get up, then sat back, startled, on the hard rocks. A sea gull had swooped in front of her so close that she could feel the touch of its wingtip. It wheeled and alighted on the rocks in front of her, standing only a few feet away, its bright eyes fixed on hers as it cocked its head back and forth.

"I'm sorry, fella," Genie said. "I don't have anything to give you. I used to bring crackers when I came here, didn't I? But you couldn't remember that. I guess a lot of people do."

The gull watched Genie for a few more minutes, then turned and studied the water below. Soon he took off, dipping down to pick up something that only his sharp eyes could see. Genie sighed and put her head down on her knees. She hadn't really been going to jump, anyway, but it was nice of the gull to stop by just when he did to give her pause, to remind her that life went on the same, day after day, and people and sea gulls had to keep going, too. But going where? What should she do? Without Byron . . .

Genie's tears began to fall, her shoulders shaking with racking sobs. "I want him back," she sobbed over and over. "I want him back." She cried until all her tears were spent, then sat and stared out over the ocean, her mind blank as she watched the waves roll in, one after another, one after another, while time seemed to stand still. She heard voices behind her, and was vaguely surprised to find that there were other people on the planet. She could not sit here forever, after all, she thought with a sigh. She would have to go back, probably to Portia's, and find out what had happened since this morning, try to make her understand. Then she would find out, somehow, where Byron was and go to him. This was no time for false pride. She would get down on her knees to him if necessary, to try to make him believe that whatever his plans for Tim, she belonged with him.

She got slowly to her feet and stood for a moment, staring down at the waves, now pounding against the rocky slope. The tide was coming in, she thought idly. She raised her head as the voices came nearer.

"There she is," said a woman's voice she didn't recognize.

"I see her," said a deep voice she knew only too well.

"Byron!" Genie gasped, whirling around. She could see him clambering rapidly up the rocks toward her, and below him, now walking away along the beach, a young girl and her companion.

"Genie! Don't move!" Byron called as his head topped the rise and he could see her face. He vaulted over one last rock and ran to her, grasping her shoulders in a viselike grip. "What in hell do you think you're doing?" he asked, his voice raw with anguish.

"I was just…standing here," she replied, staring at him in disbelief. He looked as agonized as she felt, his eyes redrimmed and sunken, a deep bloody gash along one cheek. "What happened to you?" she asked, reaching up to touch his cheek gingerly.

He shook his head dismissively. "That's nothing. The cat scratched me," he said. "You, as usual, are what happened to me." For a split second he looked furious, then suddenly his face crumpled and he crushed her against him, his cheek against hers, his shoulders shaking. "Dear God,

Genie," he choked out painfully, "don't ever frighten me like that again. I couldn't live without you."

Stunned, Genie could only hold him close, while her mind slowly began to function as it received the warmth that began in her heart and crept through her like a spring dawn. Byron hadn't run away. He was here. He cared. He had been afraid that she was going to jump off the cliff. She patted his broad back absently and rubbed her cheek against his. "There, there, love," she said softly. "Don't worry. I'm not going anywhere without you."

Byron raised his head slowly. His eyes, their thick fringes sparkling with teardrops, were burning with a new brightness. "Say that again," he said.

"I'm . . . not going anywhere without you," Genie repeated.

"No, the first part," Byron said.

At first, Genie couldn't remember. She was still so overwhelmed with relief that everything seemed unreal. Frantically she cast about in her memory for what she had said. "Do you mean, 'there, there, love'?" she asked, at last retrieving her words from their echoing space in her mind. As Byron's lips began to curve slowly into a smile she shook her head in amazement. "Didn't you know that I love you?" she asked.

"I wasn't sure," he replied, his arms tightening around her. "Didn't you know that I love you?"

"I wasn't sure, either," Genie said, tears of joy springing to her eyes. "I thought—"

"What did you think that painting meant?" Byron interrupted, his face once again unhappy. "I poured all the love in my heart into that. I thought you understood."

Genie could not bear the sight of his unhappiness. She buried her face against his chest. "I'm sorry," she said in a tiny voice. "I thought it had more to do with desire than love." She could feel Byron take in a long, ragged breath.

"That was there, too," he said. "Maybe I expected too much."

"Maybe I was still too afraid to think of love," Genie said, raising her eyes to his again. "Maybe you were, too. I thought I was pretty obvious."

They stared into each other's eyes for a long time. Then, almost as if a signal had been given, they first began to smile, then laugh. And then, with a deep groan of happiness, Byron lowered his mouth to cover Genie's and sweep the last vestiges of her misery away. She clung to his broad shoulders, feeling the wind in her hair and a song in her heart, soaring with the gulls that chorused their raucous approval above them.

"Dear God, I love you so," Byron said when at last he drew back, smiling at her radiantly. "I'll say it to you a thousand times a day from now on."

Genie blinked back the tears of happiness that insisted on filling her eyes. "A hundred or two will do," she said, sighing deeply. She felt almost guilty at feeling so joyous, for still in a corner of her heart she could feel the pain of Portia's cry, "You're no sister of mine!" She bit her lip and looked away from Byron's loving smile. Now she had to ask, and she knew it was going to hurt. She raised her eyes to his again and found him watching her intently, his smile gone.

Before she could speak, he raised his eyebrows questioningly and spoke one word. "Portia?"

Genie nodded. "I need to know..."

"Of course you do," Byron said, smiling gently. "We have a lot to talk about. Shall we go back to your house? It may take a while, and we'd be a lot more comfortable than here on this blasted rock."

"All right," Genie agreed. She had been waiting this long. She could wait a little longer.

They climbed down the jumble of rocks and walked back to the parking area, Genie cradled against Byron in the curve of his arm. "How did you find me?" she asked. "Did you just happen to be driving by and see my car?"

"Good Lord, no," Byron replied. "When I found out what had happened and discovered you were missing—" He stopped, now standing in front of the spot where their two cars were parked, side by side. "This ending up someplace with two cars has got to stop," he growled. "I'm not going off without you within reach. Lock up your car and leave it."

Genie smiled in amusement. "It is locked, but I don't think it's safe to leave it here. If you'll drive slowly..."

Byron shook his head. "Practical, but unsatisfactory. I'll send someone for it. You're coming with me. Get in." He flung the door of his Ferrari open.

With a sigh of combined frustration and pleasure, Genie got in. When Byron decided to be masterful, he was not to be denied. "Now would you tell me how you found me?" she asked when he had started his car and backed around to head for home.

"Portia gave me some ideas where I might look," he replied. "When she said you used to come here to sulk, I thought I'd try it first."

"To sulk!" Genie frowned. "I wasn't exactly sulking," she said coldly. "I felt like I wanted—" She stopped herself. There was no point in admitting how close she had come to taking the very step Byron had feared.

"I know," he said, reaching over to take her hand in his. "It's my fault. I put you and Portia through hell, when all the time my intentions were to spare both of you any of the pain. I'm sorry."

"I don't quite understand," Genie said, "but somehow I have the impression that you've talked to Portia since I did, and . . . and she's not upset anymore?" It seemed utterly impossible that Byron could have persuaded her sister to accept losing her son.

Byron shot her a desperate glance as he sped through the traffic. "Let me tell you the whole story when we get to your house," he said. "I want to be able to hold you in my arms while I tell you. And there are a few other things we need to discuss. Very important things."

"All right," Genie agreed. She managed to lean across the gap between the seats and put her head against Byron's shoulder. She closed her eyes and was startled to find that the next time she opened them they had come to a stop in her driveway, and Byron was bending over her.

"Tired, sweetheart?" he asked, gathering her into his arms.

"I'm not sure," she said, clinging to him as he carried her into the house. "Maybe just hungry. I haven't eaten anything today."

"And I suppose there's nothing in your refrigerator?" Byron looked both amused and disgusted when Genie shook her head. "My God, woman, how do you expect to keep a strapping man like me happy when you can't even feed yourself?" When Genie's eyes widened, he grinned. "I guess I got a little ahead of myself, but don't tell me you hadn't already figured out that I'm planning to marry you."

"I thought so for a while," Genie replied, "but when I discovered that moving van at your house, I gave up on that idea in a hurry. Now, would you please start to explain?"

"Not until I've ordered something to eat," Byron said firmly. He carried Genie into her bedroom, sat down with her on his lap and picked up the telephone. "Gustav," he said moments later, "send the banquet to Ms. Compton's house immediately." He gave Genie's address and then hung up the phone.

"*The* banquet?" Genie asked, frowning. "Is that all you have to say?"

"Today it is." Byron's eyes began to twinkle, and he rolled Genie onto her back and pinned her beneath him. "Now I've got you where I want you," he said, "I'll tell you everything. And after dinner—" He stopped, his eyes so bright with love that Genie caught her breath, her heart racing in anticipation.

"After dinner?" she prompted.

Byron smiled crookedly. "I guess that depends on whether you'll marry me," he said. "Will you marry me?"

"Yes," she answered simply.

Byron laid his hand along her cheek. "You're sure of that, even before you've heard what I have to tell you? You may decide I'm too much of a fool to make a good husband."

"Not a chance," Genie said, tucking her hand behind his neck and pulling him toward her. "We belong together. I'd already decided that."

"Oh, my darling love," Byron said, gathering her close and finding her lips with his. He kissed her softly at first, as if trying to hold himself back, but in only seconds a storm of passion erupted that swept them both away. Days and nights of frustrated desire boiled to the surface, coursing through eager hands that tore away clothing like winds whipping the leaves from the trees. Warm and moist, their bodies melted together. Genie heard herself making sounds of pleasure she had never made before, and felt Byron's answering caresses, sending her deeper and deeper into a world of pure ecstasy. "So wonderful," she murmured as his lips sought her breasts, and wave after wave of longing coursed through her. At last, just when she thought she could stand no more, his hand urged her to admit him and she arched eagerly to receive the thrust that would make him a part of her. Slowly and carefully he began the primal rhythm, then with increasing force, until, with an intense sound of joy, he carried her with him across the peak of ultimate release and into the valley beyond.

Spent, Byron lay quietly, his arms still holding Genie close, his cheek next to hers. She stroked his back, her eyes closed, luxuriating in the feel of his body touching hers, the scent of his hair, lying soft against her cheek. She turned her head a little and kissed him and felt him stir.

"I don't ever want to move and leave this heaven," he murmured. Then he sighed and rolled to lie beside her, smiling into her dream-struck eyes. "It was worth the wait, wasn't it?"

"More than worth it," Genie answered. "I never doubted it would be, did you?"

"Never," Byron agreed. "Although," he added with a mischievous twinkle, "there were several times I didn't think I'd last until now." His expression sobered. "And only a few hours ago, I was afraid there would never be a 'now.'"

"Tell me what happened," Genie suggested gently, "and please explain why you never told me what was going on. Wouldn't it have made things easier?"

"Probably," Byron said, cradling her in the curve of his arm and dropping a kiss on her forehead, "but if things had worked out the way they were supposed to it wouldn't have mattered. But I suppose I should start at the beginning."

"That's usually the best place," Genie said, smiling at him encouragingly. She could see from the withdrawn look that suddenly came into his eyes that in spite of his attempt to make the telling sound like a simple task, there was still something difficult for him to say.

"The very beginning," he said at last, "was the day I ran into your car. I was coming down the hill, I saw your car, and I saw two people in it. I saw you, and I saw Tim. I don't know which affected me the most. You were breathtakingly beautiful, and Tim . . . I thought I was seeing myself. I couldn't stop staring, and by the time I realized I was going to hit you, it was too late. I jerked the wheel as fast as I could, but it was no use." He grimaced. "So now you know the truth about that."

"You were so angry that I never suspected that at all," Genie said.

"Just scared," Byron said. "I'd never done anything like that before, losing all sense of where I was like that. I thought maybe I was hallucinating, since I'd been up most of the night working. Anyway, when I came back I saw that I wasn't. You were even more gorgeous—"

"I am not," Genie interrupted.

"Yes, you are," Byron said, frowning and putting his finger on her lips. "I know gorgeous when I see it. And Tim was the very image of myself as a boy, although his coloring is darker and his hair is straighter than mine was. I couldn't get either of you out of my mind. Thank God I remembered that I'd seen your name once when I was at the tennis club talking about the painting they wanted me to do.

I wanted to see you again as soon as possible and find out who Tim's parents were." He smiled crookedly as Genie bit her lip. "Are you wondering if that was the real reason I came to the party?"

Genie nodded. "I wondered for a long time if Tim was the only reason you were interested in me, especially after I saw that picture of you on your bookcase."

"It never was, but it did complicate things," Byron replied. "As soon as I found out that Tim was adopted and his mother Mexican, I called Elisa to look into the matter. She wanted to throw the de Cordova money around and bribe everyone in sight to get the answer. That was the reason I went with her to Mexico. I had to make sure she didn't create such a ruckus that she got me into legal trouble down there."

"But I thought you said she was a lawyer," Genie said.

"She is, but her usual restraint was overridden by her concern over finding out what happened to Connie's child. It took me a while to convince her that that was not my only concern, and it couldn't be hers, either. We had to think of the other people involved, too," Byron said, his fingers gently stroking Genie's hair.

"I should have guessed you'd feel that way," Genie said with a sigh.

Byron smiled wryly. "I'm sorry now that I left it for you to guess, but I wasn't as certain of things as it sounds now. After I learned that Tim's mother supposedly perished in the earthquake just as Connie did, I wanted to talk to you about it, but when you so quickly made up a story to try to divert me from even thinking about his being mine, I knew that you already had your own suspicions and would do anything to protect Portia from being hurt."

His arms tightened around Genie and he kissed her forehead softly. "I knew you'd be terribly hurt, too, if you thought there was any chance I might take Tim away from Portia. I couldn't bear the thought of hurting you that way. That was the beginning of a lot of deep thinking on my part. It would have been a difficult-enough decision, wondering if I should interfere in the life of a child who had grown up feeling he belonged to someone else. But Mark and Portia are fine people. And loving you as I did, I soon realized that no matter what I found out, I had best keep it entirely to myself. I didn't think Portia suspected anything, and I thought you'd forget it once we had our future decided. As for myself, I'd accept it as part of the past and let it go at that."

Genie laid her hand on his cheek and then caressed it gently. There were still deep lines of tension about his eyes that tugged at her sympathetic heart. "I think you underestimated me, my love," she said with gentle reproof. "I need to know what's troubling you. I want to help. I wish you'd told me."

"I wish I had now, too, sweetheart," Byron said, his arms tightening around her. "Then I'd have had you to lean on when I discovered that Tim can't possibly be my son."

Genie looked into Byron's eyes and saw a deep sorrow. "Oh, Byron, I'm so sorry," she whispered. "But he looks so much like you. How can you be sure?"

Byron sighed heavily. "Elisa went over the hospital records with a fine-tooth comb. They showed that there were three baby boys admitted after the quake. Two were claimed very shortly. The third . . . was Tim. By his name were the cryptic words 'Holy Father.' Elisa found the person who wrote that note and discovered that it meant a priest had brought him in. After that, she tracked down the

priest and got the whole story. It seems he had been shel-
tering a Salvadoran refugee family in his church. When his
church collapsed in the quake, Tim's entire family was
killed and Tim was injured. When he recovered, he was
given to the adoption agency for placement. They, apparently, never knew the entire story and hoped for a time that
his family might appear."

Genie bit her lip, feeling close to tears. "I suppose I
should be glad, and I am happy for Portia, but now you
still don't know..."

"I'll survive, sweetheart," Byron said with a little smile.
"Day by day I'm getting more used to the idea. And I think
it's better this way. I can still be Tim's favorite uncle and
enjoy watching him grow up without any of the problems
we'd have had if he were my son. Now I can concentrate on
looking forward to the children we'll have together."

Those words sent a little thrill of joy racing through Genie. "Oh, yes," she said, smiling radiantly. "You're going
to be a wonderful father."

"And you'll make a terrific mother," Byron said, his lips
grazing Genie's delicately, then claiming them with a passion that left them staring dreamily into each other's eyes.

"I guess the last thing I need to explain," Byron finally
said with a wry smile, his finger tracing Genie's face delicately, "is the mess this morning. Or maybe you'd rather
not know. It doesn't make me look terribly bright. After
all, I succeeded in making you think I'd run away and had
Portia hating both of us."

"You'd better tell," Genie said, frowning in mock se-
verity. "What on earth was that phone call from Elisa
about? That was what caused all of the trouble, wasn't it?"

Byron nodded. "That was it. Up to the very last, I'd
hoped to keep the whole thing quiet, for the reasons I

mentioned before, plus the fact that as it turned out, it made absolutely no difference to the adoption. Why should they have to bother Portia and Mark? But bureaucrats are bureaucrats, and the agency had a hard-and-fast rule that any new information had to be given to the adoptive parents. Not only that, but their letter would tell how they got the information, which would put me into the picture, which I definitely didn't want. So this morning I called Señora Ramirez, who has to be one of the most unreasonable people on earth. Elisa had told me to try a personal call, and she was already there, too, which was apparently a mistake. Mrs. Ramirez got irritated and figured we were trying to cover up something crooked, so she decided to call the Donaldsons right away. I tried to get to Portia first, but as you can guess, I didn't. And Portia completely misunderstood what Mrs. Ramirez was trying to tell her. I felt absolutely miserable about the whole thing. It took me almost an hour to get your poor sister calmed down. Anyway, it's all straightened out now. Except that I'm not sure Portia will ever forgive me for giving her such a scare.''

"Oh, I think she will," Genie said, brushing the thick dark waves back from his forehead. "She'll soon convince herself that the cosmic forces had a purpose in the whole thing. Maybe to remind her how precious Tim is to her."

"I can't imagine why they'd need to do that," Byron said with a smile. "She's the most devoted mother I've ever seen. Maybe it was to remind her how much you mean to her. After she finally calmed down about Tim, she was frantic over what she said to you on the telephone. She tried to call you to apologize, but there was no answer. It was almost eleven o'clock by then, so I came dashing up here to see if you'd left a note or, God help me, gone to my house. I knew if you'd done that, after the way I left you last night, and what Portia told you this morning, you'd have entirely the wrong idea about—"

"Just a minute," Genie said, putting her hand over Byron's mouth. "While I was trying to figure out why you left the way you did last night, I made a decision. I will not put up with any more of your cryptic remarks or your mysterious disappearances. All of this could have been avoided if you'd talked to me about it. I don't mind if you lock yourself in your studio to paint, but if we're going to have a good marriage, you're going to have to tell me what you're thinking. I can't read your mind the way you can read mine."

Byron kissed her hand and then took it away. "Oh? Then explain how you made up that story about Tim's being born in Los Angeles so quickly."

"That was an exception," Genie replied. "I usually have no idea. For instance, I can't imagine why in the world those men were moving your furniture out this morning. Why couldn't you have told me about that, so I wasn't scared to death that you'd gone?"

Byron bit Genie's finger and then grinned as she tried to frown at him severely. "It was supposed to be a good surprise, not a bad one. I'm not really crazy, just romantic. I hated that sterile, modern furniture and I could tell you didn't like it, either. We're going to do it over ourselves, and make it a nice, cozy home to raise a family in. The studio's still the same, and my bedroom. We can do that, too, but we'll need a place to sleep. What I'd planned to do, before everything got away from me, was to take you up there later this evening. I had some plans for a very romantic dinner, after which I'd put on some soft music for dancing, ask you to marry me, then, assuming that you said yes, sweep you into my arms and carry you up to bed."

"So that's why Gustav knew about the banquet. You are crazy, but I love you," Genie said, leaning up to kiss his chin. "That was a lovely idea. I'm sorry it got spoiled, but having Gustav's dinner *here* won't be too bad, will it?"

"Not bad at all," Byron smiled, kissing her briefly but passionately. "Now, where were we? Oh, Lord." He stopped and listened to the sound of the doorbell ringing. "Our dinner must be here." With a single athletic move, he leaped out of bed, grabbed the pink-flowered top sheet and wrapped it around himself like a toga. "Stay here and don't look out the window," he said as he dashed from the room, leaving Genie on the bed, giggling helplessly.

She put on her pink satin robe and waited for what seemed like a very long time, with strange bumping and thumping noises coming from her living room. At last Byron reappeared in her doorway.

"Ready, my love," he said, smiling and holding out his hand.

Genie had only stepped into the hallway when she gasped in delight. "How beautiful!" she exclaimed at the sight of an arched trellis covered with silk roses now forming the entrance from the hallway into the living room.

Byron led her through the trellis, then paused, waiting, as Genie looked around her familiar living room in a happy daze. "Like it?" he asked.

"Like it? Oh, Byron, it's just lovely," she replied, tears of happiness sparkling in her eyes as she looked up at him. The entire room was banked with potted palms and azaleas. A bouquet of roses was in the middle of the dining table, set with exquisite crystal and china.

"I was going to have my entire living room made to look like a garden," Byron said, "but I think this is even more effective. It's cozier."

"It's perfect," Genie said. "What a way to remember the day you asked me to marry you!" She flung her arms around Byron and buried her face against his neck. "I love you so much," she said.

"I adore you," he said, tilting her face up and kissing her lips softly. "Shall we sit down, or would you rather get dressed first?"

"Maybe we should," Genie said, eyeing him thoughtfully. "You look absolutely irresistible in that sheet."

"Then we shouldn't," Byron replied. "I've always wanted to be absolutely irresistible." He pulled out a chair for Genie with one hand, clutching his slipping toga with the other. "My love, do have a seat. I will open the champagne." He sat down, popped the cork and poured them each a flute of the sparkling amber liquid. "To us," he said, raising his glass.

"To us," Genie agreed. She smiled across the rim of her glass at the handsome man, wearing a pink-flowered sheet tucked beneath his muscular arms. Her heart filled with the warmth of his beautiful smile and a sudden realization that she would truly see that face across the table from her for many years to come. "I love you, Byron de Stefano," she said, "and I think we're going to have the most wonderful life together that two people ever had."

"I love you, too, my own special Genie," Byron replied. He put his glass down and eyed the still-covered dishes. "Do you suppose those would stay warm while we went back to bed for a little while?"

"Warm enough," Genie replied, setting her own glass on the table. "Shall we go?" She stood up, then laughed delightedly as Byron tossed his sheet aside and swept her into his arms. "Now you're really irresistible," she said, holding him tightly as he moved swiftly into the bedroom.

"And you are really gorgeous," Byron said, slipping her robe from her shoulders as he lowered her onto the bed. He lay down beside her and pulled her against him, then held very still, his eyes wandering lovingly over her face. "You must have been made in heaven just for me," he said. "I could never tire of looking at you."

"I feel the same way about you," Genie said, touching his cheek with her fingers. "Do you suppose Portia was right, after all? That it was kismet that brought us together that morning?"

"She told you that?"

Genie nodded. "The very first day. She also predicted only a few days later that we'd be married within the year."

"Pretty impressive," Byron said. "Has she told you yet how many children we'll have?"

Genie smiled mischievously. "No, but I think I know how to take care of that statistic."

Byron laughed as she moved against him, his arms pulling her close. "Yes, my love, I think you do," he replied.

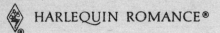

Back by Popular Demand

Janet Dailey
Americana

Janet Dailey takes you on a romantic tour of America through fifty favorite Harlequin Presents novels, each one set in a different state and researched by Janet and her husband, Bill.

A journey of a lifetime. The perfect collectible series!

December titles

#45 VERMONT
   Green Mountain Man
#46 VIRGINIA
   Tidewater Lover

HARLEQUIN ROMANCE®

is

 contemporary
and up-to-date

 heartwarming

 romantic

 exciting

 involving

 fresh and
delightful

 a short, satisfying
read

 wonderful!!

*Today's Harlequin
Romance—the traditional
choice!*

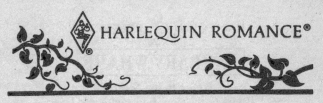

HARLEQUIN ROMANCE®

After her father's heart attack, Stephanie Bloomfield comes home to Orchard Valley, Oregon, to be with him and with her sisters.

Orchard Valley

Steffie learns that many things have changed in her absence—but not her feelings for journalist Charles Tomaselli. He was the reason she left Orchard Valley. Now, three years later, will he give her a reason to stay?

"The Orchard Valley trilogy features three delightful, spirited sisters and a trio of equally fascinating men. The stories are rich with the romance, warmth of heart and humor readers expect, and invariably receive, from Debbie Macomber."

—Linda Lael Miller

Don't miss the Orchard Valley trilogy by Debbie Macomber:

VALERIE   Harlequin Romance #3232 (November 1992)
STEPHANIE   Harlequin Romance #3239 (December 1992)
NORAH   Harlequin Romance #3244 (January 1993)

Look for the special cover flash on each book!

Available wherever Harlequin books are sold.   ORC-2

HARLEQUIN ◆ PRESENTS®

BARBARY WHARF

Home to the *Sentinel*
Home to passion, heartache and love

Charlotte Lamb

The BARBARY WHARF six-book saga continues with
Book Three, TOO CLOSE FOR COMFORT. Esteban
Sebastian is the *Sentinel*'s marketing director *and* the
company heartthrob. But beautiful Irena Olivero wants
nothing to do with him—he's always too close for comfort.

And don't forget media tycoon Nick Caspian and his
adversary Gina Tyrrell. Their never-ending arguments are
legendary—but is it possible that things are not quite what
they seem?

TOO CLOSE FOR COMFORT (Harlequin Presents
#1513) available in December.